"This is to be temporary, then, this marriage?"

"Most are, it seems to me," Luke replied harshly.

"And I take it liaisons—discreet, of course— would be acceptable." Emily watched the gleaming, predatory expression steal across his face.

"My wife won't require another lover."

He was awesome, Emily had to admit it. She was playing with fire, but it would be worth it. How dare he assume she was his for the taking?

S0-AZR-011

KIM LAWRENCE lives on a farm in rural Anglesey. She runs two miles daily, and finds this an excellent opportunity to unwind and seek inspiration for her writing! It also helps her keep up with her husband, two active sons and the various stray animals that have adopted them. Always a fanatical consumer of fiction, she is now equally enthusiastic about writing. She loves a happy ending!

Look out for Kim's next novel in Harlequin Presents, THE PLAYBOY'S MISTRESS, on sale in December.

Passionate Retribution

KIM LAWRENCE

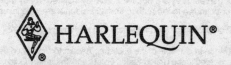

TORONTO • NEW YORK • LONDON
AMSTERDAM • PARIS • SYDNEY • HAMBURG
STOCKHOLM • ATHENS • TOKYO • MILAN • MADRID
PRAGUE • WARSAW • BUDAPEST • AUCKLAND

ISBN 0-373-80524-1

PASSIONATE RETRIBUTION

First North American Publication 2002.

Copyright © 1995 by Kim Lawrence.

This edition published by arrangement with Harlequin Books S.A.

Visit us at www.eHarlequin.com

Printed in U.S.A.

CHAPTER ONE

A DARK FIGURE silently emerged from behind a bank of luxuriant foliage and Emily let out a sharp yelp of alarm. A sliver of moonlight revealed the intruder's features and she gave a grunt of shock which she swiftly disguised as irritation. 'Must you loom like that? You almost gave me a heart attack.' She gave a frown. 'I thought you were in the Bahamas or somewhere,' she added critically. 'What are you doing here?'

'I knew you'd be delighted to see me,' a deep, gravelly voice murmured smoothly. 'How long has it been?' Emily had a glimpse of white teeth as he gave an ironic grin. 'Actually it was the Seychelles,' he corrected.

'Somewhere hot, anyway,' she agreed, brushing aside a few miles of ocean with an airy wave of her hand.

'Talking of hot, infant, why are you skulking in the conservatory?' He loosened his tie as he spoke and idly plucked a juicy grape from the vine which was trained above his head.

Emily's lips pursed in aggravation as she watched him bite the dark fruit. He had used the denigrating childhood term with benevolent scorn. Luke had always made the most of the fact that he was twelve years her senior, and as a child 'infant' had always been able to send her into an incoherent rage. She was sure that despite his negligent manner the word had been calculated; most things about Luke were calculated and his malicious humour took a continual lazy delight in mocking her own family. 'I was seeking a little privacy,' she said pointedly, refusing to notice the minor irritation. Tonight even Lucas Hunt wasn't going to spoil the euphoria of the occasion.

'It is an incredibly tedious party,' he said sympathetically. 'Don't grind your teeth like that; it's very bad for the enamel,' he advised her helpfully.

'If it's such a tedious party I don't know why you bothered coming,' she hissed back. 'No one invited you.'

'What? Miss an occasion like this—my favourite Stapely engaged to be married? It's an obligation.'

She gave a derisory hoot. 'You wouldn't recognise obligation if you fell over it; and as for being your favourite...' His opinion of her family hardly gave her cause to consider this casual comment a compliment.

'Admittedly there's not much competition: Charlotte sends me to sleep if I spend more than five minutes in her company, and your brother has the wit and charm of a waxwork. If he were similarly dumb I might be able to tolerate him, but he reveals the intellect of a bigoted bore every time he opens his mouth.'

'My sister...' Emily began, her eyes sparkling. In all sincerity she couldn't help sympathising with this opinion of her brother; his pompous smugness made it almost impossible for her to be civil to him. Fortunately their paths crossed little, but she felt instantly protective of her sister. Charlotte might be no intellectual giant but there was more to her than Luke's damning comment suggested.

'Is so two-dimensional I half expect her to disappear viewed sideways on.'

'You are incredibly snide and unpleasant to her and she suspects there's some dark, sinister meaning to everything you say.'

'And do I inspire similar inarticulate awe in you?'

'I *know* there's some dark, sinister meaning in everything you say,' she responded frankly. 'And if you've come here to spoil my night, I warn you, Luke…if you pull one of your tricks…'

Luke took a step forward and she could see his features clearly for the first time. The innocent expression should have looked absurd on the severely chiselled, swarthily dark features, but it didn't. He had changed little over the four years since she'd last seen him, unlike herself. Even if she was never going to be a raving beauty, she knew she had more to recommend her now than as the awkward, confused adolescent she had been then. Fortunately she was also now immune to the effortless charm. Mockery glittered in the intensely blue eyes. 'Tricks, Emily…?'

She clicked her tongue with disapproval recalling the occasions he'd turned up at family events, his attire and companions always geared to offend the stuffy formality. 'Are you alone?' she asked suspiciously, recalling the voluptuous actress he'd brought to her parents' silver wedding celebrations. Her father had tried so hard to avoid the lady's ample cleavage, without much success. Luke had obviously been behind the woman's embarrassingly tactile admiration of her parent, and the conveniently placed photographer who had captured the moment for the gossip column of a national newspaper the following morning…

'Straight from the plane.' He rubbed his jaw. 'Didn't even have time to shave; suffering from jet-lag. Aren't you flattered, Emmy?' He gave a long-suffering sigh. 'You little sceptic—here, feel.'

Emily was too startled to demur when he firmly placed her hand against his jaw, rubbing the pads of her fingertips against the coarse, dark growth. She blinked to banish a sudden flurry of confusion as her eyes met the intense blue regard. 'Don't be ridiculous,' she snapped, pulling her hand away. She looked pointedly at his fingers, very brown against her arm. Luke smiled slowly and released her, but not before his fingers had trailed over the blue-veined inner aspect of her wrist.

'I wish you hadn't troubled yourself on my account,' she told him, rubbing her wrist where his fingers, despite their light hold, seemed to have left a mark on her skin. She half expected to see the smudge of bruises but her flesh looked as creamily flawless as earlier.

'I shall be exemplary, an example of upright smug superiority, as befits a Stapely.'

'You are not a Stapely,' she reminded him.

'How kind of you to remind me.' A cynical smile curved his lips. 'Having seen what being a Stapely means at close quarters, I've always seen that as a cause for celebration. I seem to remember you usually accompanied that gibe with the delightful spectacle of your tongue.' His contemplative glance touched her mouth.

'I grew out of that habit,' she retorted. Did he imagine he could make her feel guilty for her childish cruelty? she wondered. All the same, it was aggravating to acknowledge that there was a sense of guilt, though heaven knew why—her infantile missiles had always glanced off him. 'I'm grown-up these days.'

The blue eyes seemed more intense as they unblinkingly examined the proof to substantiate this claim. 'Is that why you're marrying, Emmy, to prove the fact?'

Emily realised she'd been holding her breath, waiting for him to speak. Her hand went to cover her bare throat where a pulse was throbbing almost painfully. She rubbed the skin, a faint frown flitting across her face; she was curiously unsettled by the inspection. 'I feel no need to prove things, Luke, especially not to you.'

'Why especially not me?' he shot back swiftly. 'Am I special, Emmy?' His deep voice seeped honeyed mockery.

'I realise you imagine the world revolves around you but—and I know this will come as a shock—some of us make life's major decisions without considering your opinion.' Emily's lips tightened; her barbed comments had brought an almost humorous glint to his eyes.

'You're so passionate, infant, incoherently intense. Are you sure it's *you* who aren't the proper Stapely?' he drawled mockingly. 'Isn't there something a tad common about impulsive displays of emotion?'

'I believe the notion of a mix-up at the hospital was discussed,' she couldn't prevent herself commenting drily. There was little intimacy in her family and never had been; she had learnt early on that impetuous displays of warmth and affection were received, at best, awkwardly.

'What's he like, then, love's young dream?' He turned the subject, only a glimmer of a smile acknowledging her wry comment. His eyes remained beacons of cynicism.

'Am I to suppose you are for one minute interested?' Her withering look had no visible effect upon him. 'You're so bloody patronising,' she muttered, chewing her lower lip.

He raised one dark, eloquent brow and plucked another grape. 'I asked because I am mildly interested at the sort of man who has finally made you fly the nest—or rather move from one prettily feathered nest,' he amended, 'to another. Want one?' he added, holding a juicy fruit to her lips. He shrugged as she shook her head, and swallowed it himself. 'I am assuming he's not a pauper.'

'I don't know why you would assume that,' she replied coldly. Only Luke could imply that a person was an avaricious little schemer with that infuriating smile. 'What has money to do with it?' she enquired haughtily.

'Oh, not a thing,' he agreed blandly, 'when one is filthy rich.' He enlarged on the subject with smiling disdain. 'I mean, it would never occur to you to do anything as tasteless as to fall in love with a poor man, would it, sweetheart?'

He wasn't going to ruin her night, she told herself, aware of anger building steadily. He's doing it deliberately, she told herself; don't take the bait. 'I take it you've decided to despise my fiancé without having even met him,' she observed with frigid scorn.

'Some things in life have a sort of inevitability, Em. The day you decided to let your father run your life, you set a certain sequence in motion. I feel as if I've known Gavin most of my life.'

'My father does *not* run my life.'

'Come off it, Em; you've never set foot outside the cocooned abnormality of this mink-lined asylum. You've been toeing the party line ever since you could walk. Did Daddy pick out the bridegroom—or just give you a list of candidates?'

Emily sank her nails into the flesh of her soft palms to release some of the anger that made her want to lash out. How dared he breeze in here assuming he knew her every motivation? An encounter with Lucas bloody Hunt served to make her realise her good fortune in finding Gavin. He was the antithesis of Luke, she realised, mentally comparing the two men.

'Oh, I found Gavin all on my own,' she said breezily.

'Impressive. And what does Gavin do?'

Why do I feel defensive? Why shouldn't Gavin work in her family's merchant bank? she told herself, her chin tilting a few more degrees to an aggressive angle. 'Gavin works at the bank.'

'With an impeccable lineage, of course.'

'I wouldn't care if he came from a long line of bastards,' she retorted hotly. How dared he breeze in here and calmly put her on trial? She wished he'd stayed on whatever inaccessible spot he'd flown in from.

'That's very liberal of you; speaking as a first-generation bastard, I find that heart-warming.'

'I feel certain you wouldn't have allowed birth to stop you achieving that particular state. Lucas Hunt, you are a self-made...' A finger to her lips stopped her completing her sentence, and he shook his head admonishingly. She hit out with her hand, but his thumb moved to the angle of her chin, his long fingers cupping her jaw.

'I wouldn't advise it, Emmy.'

'What?' she snapped, an imminent storm flecking her eyes with gold lights. She gave an inarticulate sound of fury in her throat as her attempts to twist her head free were futile; there was tensile strength in those hands, she realised.

'Bite, isn't that the instinct that's making you grind your teeth? Bad idea,' he drawled with an indulgent sympathy that made the idea of drawing blood all the more attractive. 'How many people know that beneath that air of quiet composure lurks a little savage?'

'The only savage around here, Luke, is you,' she hissed. In fact, she found the strength of her desire to sink her teeth into his flesh vaguely shocking. 'I've no doubt you've your own reasons for being here, concern for my welfare not being one if them. I might have to tolerate your presence because my family—'

'Through a misplaced sense of loyalty won't throw me out,' he supplied with unerring accuracy. 'You don't believe that, do you, infant?' he said slowly, as his forefinger traced the outline of her full lips. 'This is a public occasion—I feel sure all the socially significant people are here, and a show of family unity is called for. No matter how much Charlie would love to throw me out of Charlcot, he won't.'

With a sense of quiet desperation she shook her head and much to her relief Luke released her; the tactile sensation had been intimidating out of all proportion to the casual contact. It must be the tension of the whole occasion, she told herself; it was far too elaborate, not at all the quiet, intimate celebration she had wanted. But Gavin had sided with her family on this occasion until she'd felt it churlish not to go along.

'I suppose you think being something of a celebrity

makes your presence indispensable,' she sneered, willing her pulse-rate to return to its normal level. She ignored the undoubted accuracy of his observation; in public, at least, her family would accept Luke.

'Being a publicly recognisable face means more to your father than it does to me. Not only does he have to accept me publicly, he actually has to project pride.' The smile was cruelly complacent. 'You find it more comfortable to accept things on face value, don't you?' he said with contemplative distaste. 'You've acquired a veneer of unpleasant hypocrisy, Emily.'

'It's you who continues this feud, a remnant of some childish grudge. Don't you think it's about time you forgot the past? I don't care what you think of me, but none of it has anything to do with me,' she said wearily. The constant warring repelled her; there was something so single-minded, almost malignant, about Luke's derisive contempt.

'While your name is Stapely, Em, you *are* involved,' he said, a harsh inflexion in his voice.

'Then the fact I'm about to change my name should please you: one less Stapely for you to hate!' she yelled. A sudden frown. 'You don't seem exactly overjoyed at my impending nuptials,' she said, puzzled, as it occurred to her that he was displaying uncharacteristic interest.

Luke shrugged, his long, lean body relaxed in contrast to her tense posture. The hooded eyelids half shielding the brilliant blue gaze gave the impression of boredom. 'Do you require universal approval for peace of mind, Em? Surely a few home truths from me can't matter. Can it be that there are doubts lurking in that delectable heaving breast? Are there?'

'They don't... You don't... Not that they are true, of course,' she amended somewhat incoherently. The direction of his gaze made the colour rise in her face. 'You have a distorted view of everything,' she protested. Something on the periphery of her vision distracted her. She tore her eyes from the ironic blue gaze. At the same instant it occurred to her that it could appear strange if she emerged from the shrubbery with anyone other than her fiancé, especially if the other turned out to be Luke. She heard the sound of said fiancé's voice and gave a grimace; she wished she hadn't waited guiltily for those few silent moments—she should have revealed her presence immediately.

She didn't look up at Luke; she was sure he would take the opportunity to make the situation as awkward as possible. Not that Gavin would believe for an instant anything but the most innocent of explanations; unlike Luke, he didn't have a cynical, distorted view of human nature.

'We shouldn't, Gavin.'

Emily froze in the act of stepping forward.

'We've got to tell her, Charlotte.' The sound of soft cries of distress and the unmistakable murmurs of exchanged embraces hung in the humid air.

Emily felt strangely objective, as if what she was listening to had nothing to do with her: it was as impersonal as a radio drama. It wasn't her fiancé and her sister exchanging what sounded like a wildly passionate embrace, but two strangers and studio effects. The sound of her own breath sounded unexpectedly loud in her ears, accompanied by the thud of her heartbeat.

'It's no good, Gavin, we can't do this to Emmy…she's my sister.' Emily heard her sister's soft voice crack with emotion and the sound of soft sobs filled the room.

A mental scream was building in her head; this was real…it was actually happening. Her head felt as if it would explode; there was no vocal outlet for the anguish that swiftly flowed through her ruthlessly. With my own sister… The words went around in her head. Not Charlotte, she prayed uselessly, the concept was too awful to contemplate, but it was true. Gavin's reply left no room for doubt.

'But it's you I want, darling.'

'I couldn't, knowing I'd wrecked Emmy's happiness. I couldn't live with that.'

Emily touched her cheek, surprised to find it wet with tears. Teeth clamped over her lower lip, she closed her eyes. She couldn't live with it, poor Charlotte, she thought bitterly. Charlotte was a fraud. Anger mixed with an acute nausea surged through her in violent waves. It seems a little late for regrets, sister, dear.

'But I need you...'

She had never heard that inflexion in Gavin's voice; she wished she hadn't heard it now. The pain was intense, and humiliation more profound than anything she had encountered before confronted her like a solid object. It jolted into life a long-forgotten memory, just as an odour could conjure up some distant recollection of a time, a place, an event consigned to the dim recesses of memory.

'Emily needs you.'

She shook her head free of the scarlet fingernails running through the dark hair of the tall man. The image was startlingly vivid. Her mind returned to her sister's soft pink nails and her fiancé's blond hair. The pain was acute; it stimulated her senses, and she was conscious of every nuance in the voices; her ears, strained to hear, could imagine every gesture, every touch.

'Emily needs someone to agree with her.' Bitterness was unmistakable and she bit her lip to stop the sound of distress which obstructed her throat. 'She never actually listens to me.'

The duplicity was like a physical blow. He was angry with her... The irony tasted bitter in her dry mouth. She couldn't listen to any more; she felt as if the walls were closing in around her. With her hands clamped over her ears she ran towards the open door that led out on to the terrace, past caring if they heard her.

The soft evening air hit her after the hothouse atmosphere of the emotion-clogged room she'd fled from. She hit the turf running and didn't stop until her lungs complained too fiercely. She sank down on to her knees and her head fell forward, spreading her honey-brown hair around her. A touch on the exposed nape of her neck made her start and raise her tear-stained, turbulent features.

'Go away!' she spat venomously. The last thing she needed right now was any of Luke's barbed comments. What had happened was bad enough, but that Luke of all people had heard every humiliating syllable was the crowning glory.

He met the tear-drenched, golden-brown eyes, shot with gold as they always were when she was in the grip of strong emotion, impassively. 'OK,' he agreed after a short pause.

She watched as he turned, his long-legged stride, peculiarly elegant, swallowing up the ground. 'No, don't go…'

He turned. 'You need a whipping-boy?' he asked, one dark eyebrow quirking.

'Well, if it's sympathy I'm after I wouldn't be turning to you, would I?' she snapped back. She sniffed loudly; the instinctive words needed an explanation, and she was glad he'd supplied it because she couldn't. Why cling to Luke's company? She pushed her heavy hair back from her face and straightened the skirt of her heavy silk dress. 'Grass stains all over,' she said, wondering why she was discussing the state of her clothes when her whole future lay in shreds around her…

How could they? Outraged horror blinded her to her surroundings; she forgot the man standing contemplating her limp, distraught figure with enigmatic eyes. How long had they been…? They had been lovers…they *were;* some instinct told her this. The intimacy had been in their voices.

She recalled Gavin's smiling face as her parents had toasted them earlier; nothing in his exterior had given any clue to the infidelity which even then he—they—must have been plotting and scheming. Had he continued with the charade because he hadn't been totally sure of Charlotte? Am I a reserve? she wondered furiously.

Luke reached her side. He held out a hand to heave her to her feet. 'In that dress, Emily, no one's eyes stray as far as the skirt,' he assured her. His eyes were fixed unapologetically on the upper slopes of her breasts, which gleamed above the stark black fabric of her strapless gown.

'Not everybody has such a sordid mind as you,' she told him. The sexual innuendo was peculiar: nothing like that ever entered their relationship…friendship would be stretching it to breaking-point, though he wasn't always as unpleasant as he had been this evening. Luke sparred with her, baited her, tried and occasionally succeeded in shocking her, but nothing intimate. Even in her present state of miserable confusion she registered that she didn't care for that brief comment, made more to distract her than for any other reason, she was sure. Was that Luke's idea of kindness? His next words firmly contradicted this concept and made her catch her breath.

'If you find a healthy admiration of a good cleavage sordid, maybe that's why lover boy has looked elsewhere,' he suggested unsympathetically.

She felt torn between a strong desire to collapse into tears of pain, and violent outrage at the heartless comment. The brilliant blue regard was as cold and indifferent as ice; pride made her face him without a quiver in her voice, and a sense of self-preservation kept her hands firmly at her sides. The pleasure of striking him would be diluted by the fact that he would undoubtedly retaliate in kind; she'd tried that in the dim and distant past and some things never changed.

'My sex life is none of your business.'

'Just as well—I have such a lamentably low boredom threshold,' he said silkily.

'You're enjoying this,' she accused, her voice shaking. 'I have just…'

'Found out your boyfriend prefers the big sister,' he provided helpfully as she took several deep breaths. He gave a shrug of his broad shoulders. 'Why worry? You heard her about to make the supreme sacrifice on the altar of sisterly love.' He made a noise of disgust. 'I thought I was going to throw up. All you have to do is keep quiet.'

'You think I would?' she gasped incredulously.

He regarded her thoughtfully. 'Actually, I thought you would have waded in and thrown the odd left hook. You do have a very tactile temperament, Emmy,' he recalled reflectively.

Luke had an odd expression on his face that she couldn't decipher, but then, he was fairly expert at not revealing what he was thinking; he'd honed the craft over the years until he could easily blanket his emotions under a bland smile or a rock-like impassivity that could be infuriating. But then, it was usually intended to be just that...

Something about the way he said 'tactile' made a shiver run down her spine: his rough velvet voice managed to make the word sound oddly voluptuous.

'These days I actually think things out before reacting,' she replied huskily. This was all some extra amusement as far as he was concerned, a chance to see a Stapely suffer a little. Luke had never made any effort to hide his contempt for the entire family, and she couldn't suppose she was an exception.

'Pity, I always found your spontaneity abrasively refreshing. Possibly your Gavin has been encouraging all these latent and unattractive aspects of your character. An awful thought offers itself, infant; you could be turning into your mother.'

She listened impassively to his soft drawl. It occurred to her that it was bizarre that he was the one she'd called back in a moment of supreme crisis. It couldn't even be considered clutching at straws because, with Luke, a person could never be sure whether he'd hold you under or pull you out—his motivation remained a mystery even though she'd known him all her life. A sure sign of mental instability, she told herself with self-derision, actively to seek his company. Shouldn't she have flung herself in maternal arms? Actually she never had done; there was always the possibility that she might have messed Mummy's dress or mussed her hair. As for announcing that she was about to call off the engagement... Emily gave a laugh at the idea. Her mother would consider such an idea, for whatever reason, the height of insanity. What would people think...?

'What's so funny?'

Emily almost told him; he'd have appreciated the joke. Appearances must be maintained at all costs! But when she thought about it, it wasn't really funny.

'Life's irony?' she suggested, throwing her arms wide expansively. 'Well, at least it's all made your effort worthwhile. Think of the chaos when I announce a wedding will not take place!'

Luke sat down on a fallen tree and she realised for the first time that her flight had taken her as far as the riverbank; the house was a glitter of lights through the trees. 'You aren't even going to fight for him, then?'

'Fight?' she echoed. 'He wants my sister,' she reminded him in a choked voice. The reminder of this fact made her stomach churn; all the familiar landmarks of her life seemed to have disappeared, and the landscape seemed unfamiliar and frightening. Have I been blind? she asked herself. The anger, directed partly at herself, sent her adrenalin into overdrive. She began to pace restlessly over the damp grass. The lies, the deceit... What had been the truth? Had he ever cared for her?

She wrung her hands in anguish, her fingers growing bone-white as the action cut off her blood supply. 'It must be a mistake,' she muttered, half to herself, no conviction in her voice, just a sense of desperation. I spend weeks coming to the most momentous decision in my life... That makes my judgement—what? Disastrous hardly seemed sufficient, she thought bitterly.

'Come off it, Emily, there has been nothing inadvertent going on here. Your Gavin knew exactly what he was doing—and Charlotte, despite the tears and sickly remorse, did too. They knew they were wrong but they did it anyway,' he reminded her brutally.

'Considering my earlier defence of Gavin, you must be feeling pretty smug,' she replied. The fury that sought an outlet was in her face as she turned on her heel and glared at him accusingly. 'Anyone would think I'd *expect* deceit by now—God knows I'm surrounded by it every day of the week. My parents' marriage is purely window-dressing...' Her marriage was going to be different, she... Wrong tense, she mentally corrected herself.

'Believe it or not, when I spoke earlier I wasn't expecting such a dramatic revelation,' he returned drily. 'The question is, what are you going to do? Are you going to fight for him, Emmy?' he persisted.

Her eyes focused on his face, surprised by his question and the unusual tone in his voice. 'I don't want him.'

'You love him?'

'Don't be absurd—I was about to marry him!'

'Not the same thing; people marry for lots of reasons.'

He brushed a stray leaf from the dark fabric of his trousers, and watched her from beneath his thick lashes, the only concession in his features to anything not abrasively masculine.

'Charlotte loves him,' she said in a choked voice.

'At least you can allow the full wrath of Charlie to fall on her head; you, sweetheart, are in the clear. You are the injured party and Charlotte is the bad guy... You do realise she won't be able to survive the guilty bliss at the expense of her sister's? the martyrish instinct is too deeply ingrained.'

She frowned at his sneering tone but realised the truth in his words. She felt a certain savage satisfaction. 'Good!'

'Who says charity begins at home?' he remarked drily.

'Am I supposed to make a present of him, gift-wrapped? *I'm* the injured party here,' she reminded him, her eyes flashing.

'And I'm sure you'll be universally sympathised with once the sordid details get out. Sweet revenge on big sister, and it's not even as if you love him, is it?'

His words were like a slap in the face; they ricocheted around the small clearing. 'How dare you—?' she began.

'Save the schoolmarm tone for those who are intimidated by it, infant,' he advised softly. 'Your sister just filched your property and the boyfriend just trampled all over your pride, and it hurts like hell; but you're not reacting like a girl whose heart is broken, so don't expect any sympathy from me.'

He was the most insensitive, wantonly cruel man on the face of the earth, she decided. 'I must say I find it amusing to hear you speak about love as if you're the expert. Thirty-two and unmarried might make some people draw conclusions,' she suggested outrageously.

Luke took this slur on his manhood unblinkingly. 'I could see over the potted palms,' he said softly, recalling the recent scene in the conservatory and the advantage of his six feet three compared to her average stature. 'Pretty boy—is that what made you pick him out to propagate the species?'

'I'm not as preoccupied with a pretty face as you appear to be.'

'That's a rather bizarre avenue for you to take just to avoid a simple question,' he said, standing up in that fluid way he had of moving. The grace and co-ordination of a jungle cat, she realised, momentarily diverted; strength masked by totally misleading indolence. Looking at his face, seeing no sign of anger at her comment, just an even more frightening absence of expression that was inhumanly cold, she wrapped her arms around herself, suddenly aware of the chill of the night.

'Could you be asking me to offer proof of my masculinity?' he asked, as though he were discussing the weather.

'L-Luke!' she stuttered, alarmed at his response to her unthinking gibe. It had never occurred to her that Luke was in any way effeminate; the idea was incredibly absurd! She'd just been hitting back without considering the fact that this target was unlikely to sit still and take the abuse. 'Now who's being absurd?' she said, trying to sound firm and in control of the situation.

'Male vanity is a very tender thing, Emmy,' he purred, taking, much to her alarm, another step in her direction. 'It should be nurtured.'

'Tender my foot; you're as fragile as the average steel bar, and about as insensitive too.' The idea that she could pierce his impenetrable hide made her realise he had to be reacting like this just to frighten her. If she had been less distracted she'd have realised this straight away. She knew him, of course, but it occurred to her that the knowledge she had was quite superficial.

He'd been at school when she had been a small child—with her own brother, Paul, but not of course at the same school. A second-class school was as far as her father's obligation to his adoptive cousin's child went. It wasn't as if she'd actually been real family, he was fond of reminding them at frequent intervals. Luke's mother's background had been a mystery. How had she repaid their generosity? With Luke, a cruel but, in her father's eyes, predictable outcome to such a foolish action. She had rejected all the advantages bestowed upon her and had chosen to raise her son single-handed, turning her back on the adoptive parents who had rejected her. It had of course been a source of intense frustration to her parents when Luke, the cuckoo in the nest, had outshone their own cosseted heir in every field. Both young men had gone on to the same university, but Luke had gone on a scholarship and her brother had scraped in.

Her brother, while not her favourite person, was still her brother and her attitude to Luke owed much to his resentment. He'd slaved away, at least so he'd told them, and Luke had mixed with undesirable elements, getting involved in numerous dissident activities, and had still managed to emerge the other side with a first. The details to her young mind had meant little, but she could understand the seething frustration and dislike her brother had felt.

In retrospect, she was glad Luke had incredibly refused the offer of a post in the merchant bank her grandfather had created. He had never fitted snugly into her world; their relationship was tenuous; he was a connection rather than family. Even without the blood tie it made him the proverbial black sheep, who hadn't had the decency to be a failure. At the time it had caused a minor furor. 'After all we've done for him' and 'bad blood will out' had been two phrases she recalled being bandied about a good deal. But at least Paul hadn't had to start his career under the shadow of his cousin's flair and undoubted ability.

At the time it had been decided and, she suspected, fervently hoped that Luke would regret his arrogant assumption that he could make his own way without the cushioning security of the family. He hadn't, of course, and, though his visits were not frequent, he kept in touch as much to flaunt his success as his unconventional lifestyle which was anathema to her tradition-bound household.

It hit her in that split-second as she opened her mouth to denounce Luke's tactics and total lack of feeling. The corrosive impact of all she had lost in a few moments made her fight for air and go deathly pale. All her dreams...plans. And the humiliation. How long had they...? She tormented herself with the knowledge that while she had discussed the wedding plans with Charlotte, her sister had been... She closed her eyes, a deep cry of distress wrenched from her throat.

'Don't faint!' The voice sounded faintly impatient and the hands that forced her into a sitting position and pushed her head between her knees were ruthlessly efficient but not very gentle.

Emily took several deep gulps and the singing in her ears retreated to the distance. She raised her head cautiously.

'I never had you pegged as the swooning sort.'

She glared hazily at the harsh features of her companion and swore. 'It's not every day I find my boyfriend prefers my sister. I realise vulnerability isn't a familiar term to you,' she snarled. Considering that the first book he'd published had made her weep unashamedly, he really was the most inhumane person she had ever met. She recalled the stark black and white pictures, each with a few succinct and touching lines illustrating, without the need of lengthy dialogue, the inequality between the children scattered over the globe, their fates sealed by the arbitrary hand of geography.

'You'll get over it.'

This announcement made her abandon her attempt to puzzle the paradox of Luke's personality; the depth of sensitivity and compassion for human vulnerability she'd seen in those pictures, and the cynical man who had the viperous tongue and barbarous humour with which he heartlessly annihilated others with what seemed like arbitrary cruelty. 'That's the future; it's now I'm concerned about.' Her confused eyes collided with the startling blue gaze, not expecting to find an answer to her dilemma. 'What am I going to do?' she said bleakly, half to herself.

'No one's going to blame you.'

She blinked, hurt by the unspoken implication that she was in some way to blame. The innuendo in his voice she could normally cope with, but her emotions felt too close to the surface, vulnerable to every nuance. 'I suppose that's what everyone will think—it was my fault that he went with Charlotte. I can see it now. I wasn't woman enough…' The knowing glances, the speculation and the pity too. 'I don't want pity.'

'I won't give you any,' he assured her. 'It seems to me you're indulging in just about all you can handle. I hope you don't mind my pointing it out, Emily, but when you start to wallow in self-pity you get this unattractive whining note in your voice.' He patted her head. 'You might keep it in mind.'

She flinched away furiously. 'You are loathsome…a reptile,' she told him with deep conviction.

He grinned, not noticeably daunted by the announcement. 'I'm only trying to be helpful.'

'Then go walk under a bus,' she said childishly. The moment the words were out she realised what she had said. 'Oh, God! I didn't mean…' Agitated, her hand went to her mouth. 'I was just…'

'You think it might be hereditary, do you, infant? I assure you I have no suicidal tendencies at present.'

'You can't know it was suicide.' For a moment her own dilemma receded, and she rushed on, anxious to redress any unintentional wound she'd inflicted. 'Your mother was ill, the witnesses couldn't tell whether she fell or, or…' Her eyes slid away from the sapphire gaze.

'Stepped out deliberately,' he supplied without a hint of emotion in his voice. 'My mother stepped out all right.'

'Luke, you can't know,' she protested, instinctively reaching out and clasping his arm.

His eyes were hard and his expression sombrely composed—the combination made her heart thud painfully as he looked directly at her. 'She stepped out, but it wasn't suicide…it was murder, Emily,' he continued, ignoring her horrific gasp. 'Your father killed her as surely as if he'd driven a knife into her heart, in fact, the latter would have been kinder.'

She stepped back a pace. 'That's a wicked thing to say.'

'My dear Emmy, you don't even begin to know the meaning of the word. There is wickedness out there.' He made an expansive gesture. 'Enough to kill your dreams, invade your very soul.' She made a sound of protest; the blankness in his eyes was something she didn't want to see. Then, as if a veil had slipped back into place, the crooked, cynical grin was back and she almost welcomed the normality. 'The major catastrophe in your life is the fact you've been made a fool of. I've watched and reported bloodbaths and atrocities that make me feel nothing, so if you're looking for sympathy...' His eyes glittered with a dispassionate mockery.

'Compared to some things I realise this is petty and trivial, but I'm not feeling global disaster—just personal disaster,' she said, strangely calmed by his brief, shocking and totally uncharacteristic outburst. Did Luke have his vulnerabilities? The concept was alien. All the time she'd known him she'd never seen him come off worst in any encounter; he had always had that callous contempt for authority and an apparently limitless belief in his own ability.

She brushed down her long skirt and raised her eyes to his face. Life had hardened, not mellowed, Lucas Hunt, but experiences beyond her imagination had obviously left their mark. The blue eyes stared back and Emily shivered; the mental picture she'd established over the years of Luke seemed for a moment out of focus. She had the strangest sensation of looking at a stranger...as strangers went, he would have been worth several covert looks.

'The search parties will be out looking for me,' she said giving herself a brief mental shake. There were more pressing matters to concentrate on than Lucas Hunt. She lifted her skirt above the damp grass and walked up the incline towards the house.

'What are you going to do?' Luke had fallen into step beside her, but she chose to ignore him.

'I don't know yet,' she admitted.

'No grand scheme?'

'I'm waiting for inspiration,' she informed him honestly. No magical solution had crystallised in her head; in fact, she felt that things were bound to get a whole lot worse this evening. She felt fatalistic about the whole event. 'I don't know why you're following me. I mean, trivial domestic dilemmas are all a bit beneath you, aren't they?'

'Morbid curiosity?' he suggested, steadying her arm as she slipped on the damp turf. She snatched it away angrily. 'I'm waiting to see inspiration strike. I'm sure it'll be enlightening.'

CHAPTER TWO

THEY ENTERED by a side-door. Emily felt physically sick now that the confrontation she could so well imagine was imminent.

Gavin, why did you do it? The question kept going around in her head. He had seemed genuinely fond of her—in fact, his devotion had been vaguely embarrassing at times. He was everything she could have wanted in a husband: he was considerate, kind, bright and, compared to the men in her own family, incredibly sensitive to her feelings. The novelty of having her wishes considered paramount had been original, a heady feeling of being cherished and one she felt sure she could tolerate on a permanent basis.

As for Charlotte, the thought of her sister made her feel wretched, trust betrayed... She didn't know when, if ever, she would be able to trust herself actually to confront her and remain even moderately civilised.

'I wish you'd go away.' She looked in Luke's direction, transposing some of her anger on to his able shoulders. The barely restrained vitality he was fairly oozing was an added insult. It was reflected in the way he moved, the air of expectation... He was enjoying it, she realised with fury. Contemplating her distress seemed to act on him in a stimulating way, so stimulating that she felt a fresh spasm of unease. At least, she reassured herself, she could be sure of one thing: not even Luke could make things worse at the moment.

'I'm here to lend you my support.'

'Why doesn't that make me feel better—?' she wondered out loud. She broke off as they both heard the sound of voices at the selfsame instant. A door opened and the throb of music filtered into the small hallway. 'I can't... I don't think I can cope with this.' Blind panic that had made her freeze for an instant suddenly sent urgent life into her limbs. 'I've got to...' She had to run, get away. Eyes wild with the urgent drive to escape, she searched the room for an avenue of escape.

Fresh shock swept through her veins, interwoven with a snowballing sense of panic, when without warning Luke turned towards her, trapping her between the wall and his body. Impressions were bombarding her brain as she tried to think beyond the immediate impact which made her laboriously gasp for air, her head growing immediately light.

He was a large man, not heavily built but muscular and hard. She hadn't actually appreciated the physical proportions of his tall, rangy frame previously. He was close enough without being in actual physical contact for her to be aware of the heat of his body and the male odour which emanated from him, a clean smell, not tainted by the overuse of scents and potions. Unconsciously her hands went out, palms outwards to preserve her own space.

'You're hyperventilating,' he observed impatiently, looking down into her alarm-filled face.

'What are you...?'

'Inspiration, remember? That's what I'm here to provide. And if you want to get out of this mess with some of your precious pride intact, just follow my lead,' he told her harshly. He bent his dark head and she closed her eyes with a sense of impending doom.

Inspiration obviously allowed for no preliminaries, because she found her hands flattened against the hard plane of his belly as he pressed forward, pinning her to the wall with his weight. She wasn't aware of one hand sliding beneath her hair to cup her skull, but she found her move-

ments being controlled by the touch of his fingers. She
breathed his name, filled with an intense desire to escape;
but the sound of her voice was lost against the movement
of his mouth.

Luke was kissing her. The concept was too strange to
grasp completely. She stood stock-still, counting the sound
of her own laboured inhalations. The awareness of his
heavy thighs pressing against her traumatised her already
impaired nervous system.

'Open your mouth, infant.' His voice was tinged with
heavy exasperation.

What the hell did he think he was doing, hauling her
about like a doll and handing out ridiculous instructions as
though she were some sort of puppet? She opened her
mouth to tell him exactly what he could do, but he seemed
to take this as compliance. The abrupt intimacy of his
tongue colliding with her teeth, touching the moistness of
her inner lip, was like a bolt of pure, intense excitement. It
destroyed all coherent thought processes—and most physical responses too. The weakness was totally debilitating,
and if his hands hadn't slid across her back she would have
slid to the floor at that moment.

Nothing in her life had prepared her for the black hole
of pure sensation she found herself sinking into. Countering
the sensation never entered her head; the intensity required
total co-operation. She let the flow carry her along. She
was absorbed in the texture of his lips against her tender
mouth in a way that was totally alien. A kiss was something
pleasant, if you were lucky in your partner, but something
she had been able to stop without the wrenching feeling of
loss she experienced when Luke raised his head.

She stared at him in a half-horrified, half-fascinated way
before she registered the sound of her own father's voice.
The blue eyes held an ambiguous mingling of mockery and
anger. Why should Luke be angry? she wondered. *I* should
be angry... I *am* angry.

'What do you think you're doing?'

Luke moved to one side after winking at her, his expression contemplative but palpably unmoved by the ardent embrace. The realisation was painfully humiliating. 'Charlie, I would have thought that was rather obvious,' he said, smiling with silky provocation. His fingers strayed seemingly automatically to Emily's bare shoulder, his fingers stroking her hot skin.

At any other time her father's thunderstruck expression of total incredulity would have made her laugh. She felt just as stunned herself; her bemused brain was only just beginning to function. Her father's mouth was open, his face suffused with a purplish glow that stood out in violent contrast to the leonine mane of silver hair he was so proud of. He wasn't supposed to get over-excited, some sane portion of her brain recalled fuzzily.

'Hello, Father,' she said stupidly. The tableau had to be broken at some point and Luke appeared to be savouring each moment too much to be of any assistance. She couldn't look at Luke—what little dignity she had left he'd managed to rip into shreds. She would murder him, slowly, painfully and with relish! she decided.

'What are you doing with him…?' His eyes touched Luke with an expression of loathing. He seemed to be noticing details that he hadn't done previously: the torn, mud-stained dress, her tangled hair. Details that Emily had not until that moment been conscious of herself. The picture must be pretty damning.

She lifted a trembling hand to her lips, which felt bruised and tender—no doubt as Luke had intended. She felt a small bud of anger blossom dramatically as her breast swelled with a sense of victimisation. Did he imagine for one moment that she'd agree to such a transparently ludicrous ploy to extract her from her engagement and save face? As for his mauling her about in quite such a realistic fashion, she'd never forgive him, ever, even if it was for her father's benefit.

Not that she was about to lose any sleep over a kiss, she told herself stubbornly. Lurking in her mind was a growing sense of unease at the devastating response of her normally co-operative senses. With forewarning, she told herself, throwing Luke a fulminating glance, I could have taken the thing in my stride. Luke smiled back at her, allowing the hard lines of his face to dissolve into something more warm, more intimate.

'Emily was putting me out of my misery, Charlie,' Luke said, a throb of emotion in his voice. Staring into the very blue eyes, Emily felt a twinge of pity for any female he turned the charm on, for it would be awfully difficult not to believe the apparent sincerity he could infuse into his expression.

'I wasn't talking to you,' Charles Stapely snarled, his expression growing even uglier as Luke brushed the stray strands of hair from her brow tenderly.

Emily forced herself to accept his ministrations passively, but she longed to push his fingers away. The sensation was disagreeable; it made the muscles low in her belly clench in objection and she was filled with a restless sense of unease that she was sure was associated with the contact. She was going to stop this farce now—anything was preferable, she thought, shuddering.

His lips brushed her ear. 'What do you prefer, infant victim?' he murmured, his voice low but perfectly distinct. Their eyes met. 'Or fallen woman,' he mouthed silently but distinctly.

The internal battle was violent but brief. Luke had forced her into this absurd charade from the worst of motives, she had no doubt; but he had given her this choice. The sympathy, the knowing glances...

'I realise this must be a shock, Father,' she said. Luke smiled, complacent and unsurprised. He had known her weakness all along, the pity she couldn't stomach. He foiled her attempt to move away by encircling her waist with his arm. His hand moved restlessly over her silk-clad midriff and she felt her thoughts telescope together, and her next comment slipped out of reach. It was at the same time a jarring but soothing sensation, Luke's fingers over the soft fabric. Soothing... I must be mad, she decided as the thought surfaced.

'The fact is, Charles, Emily knew how you would react to—' his eyes sought hers for a brief moment as if they were exchanging some profound secret. '—us,' he said, his expression sincere as he looked at the older man. Emily silently wondered at the proficient way he lied; the more outrageous the claim, the more convincing he appeared. If she hadn't been busy loathing him she might almost have admired the talent. 'She got involved with Gavin to forget me, but some things...'

Emily gasped. That was going just a bit far even for her father to swallow. But, looking at Luke's profile, she thought perhaps he didn't want her father to be convinced; he was laying things on with a trowel, deliberately letting the older man know that he had in some way engineered this event—which, of course, he had. Things were slipping from her control like sand through her fingers. Luke was putting an alarming amount of effort into his part, and the malice he was directing at her father was painfully obvious.

While she wasn't close to either of her parents, she felt uncomfortable at colluding with Luke to further his campaign.

'In the circumstances, I can't really continue with my engagement,' she said softly. The way both men looked at her made her realise they had both forgotten her existence for a split-second. 'So glad to see I have your attention,' she said sweetly, filled with a revitalising wrath. 'There was nothing intentional in this, Father, and with all due respect I feel I should discuss this with my...with Gavin first. I know you've gone to a lot of trouble and expense,' she added drily, even if she had begged for a simple affair to announce her engagement. The lavish occasion had not been of her seeking. 'It's better to discover these things now,' she said, wincing at the triteness of the phrase that rolled off her lips.

'How true,' Luke breathed blandly in her ear. 'You are so deep, infant.'

Emily matched her expression to his, her features arranged in slavish adoration, a besotted smile on her lips. 'Move it or lose it,' she said, referring to his hand which had strayed to her behind.

Luke gave a deep growl of laughter and didn't comply with her hissed command.

Her father hadn't had the benefit of hearing the content of this brief interchange, but he had endured the apparent intimacy of the low-voiced murmurs. He gave a bitter laugh, his expression a mixture of spite and scorn as he looked at his daughter.

'Unintentional?' he yelled scornfully. 'If you believe that you're even more stupid than I thought. You don't suppose he—' he flicked Luke a look of abhorrence, '—would have wasted his time on you if you weren't my daughter? A man like Gavin is worth a hundred of him. You'll live to regret this, Emily, and in the not too distant future,' he warned. 'You won't let the past die, will you?' he said, his attention once more on the other man.

'I always keep my promises, Charlie,' Luke said softly. 'Opportunities arise, and wasn't it you who always advocated grabbing them with both hands?'

'You admit it, then?' Charles asked hoarsely.

'Father, calm down, please,' Emily said urgently. The distended vein that throbbed in his temple made her stomach tighten in alarm. She'd known even without Luke's contribution just how angry her father was going to be; this had always been a damage-limitation exercise, but it was getting out of hand.

'Shut up!' He rounded on her. 'I'll deal with you, later.'

'Your heart…' she began anxiously. She had to tell him the truth. Perhaps that wouldn't seem so bad after this charade. It was selfish of her to save her own pride at the risk of her father's health, she decided, contemptuous of her own weakness in accepting Luke's get-out clause.

'There's nothing wrong with my heart, you idiot,' he spat back contemptuously.

Emily was immobilised by a thrust of confused pain. 'But…'

'I wouldn't have thought you'd care if I dropped dead at your feet.'

Emily had seen the swift dart of panic in her father's eyes, and the truculent observation did nothing to diminish an awful feeling that was solidifying in her head. 'You just said there was nothing wrong with your heart.'

'Why would you think there was, infant?' Luke had been watching this interchange with sharp interest.

'He has a heart condition.'

'Don't you dare discuss family matters with him!' Was there a hint of desperation in the blustery tone?

I heard the doctor tell him. It was an accident; I wasn't meant to. She spoke inaudibly, her lips moving silently. As she tried to unravel the impossibility of her awful suspicion, Emily had the feeling that her mental processes were not as acute as they might have been. 'I wasn't supposed to hear.' She spoke out loud. Horror entered the eyes she fixed unwaveringly on her father's face. 'Was I?' The timing had been so perfect, so convenient.

Belligerence entered Charles Stapely's face. 'You've been contaminated by that swine already…my own daughter.'

She'd been about to leave home, set up her own flat. The initial opposition had been fierce; her father had Victorian ideas about a female's place and role in society. He wanted her where he could keep his eye on her, control her. Persuading him had been a futile task but short of incarceration he couldn't prevent her; and, much to her surprise, he had suddenly capitulated, given her his blessing. She'd been on cloud nine—her first job as a probationary primary-school teacher and a small flat of her own.

Even after she'd overheard his conversation with the doctor he'd insisted with untypical generosity that she mustn't let the frailty of his condition stop her living her life.

She'd had a few moments alone with the apparently eminent heart specialist. No, the only treatment possible was conservative, he'd told her, no surgery. Stress could contribute and hasten the inevitable, he'd agreed when she'd tentatively enquired. The words had shocked her, made her realise the gravity of her father's condition.

He'd been grateful that she decided to stay, almost tearful; it was one less thing for him to worry about, he'd told her. At that time he'd sworn her to secrecy; one word of his condition and the bank could be compromised. He'd promised to take life easier, but she could understand and even admire his determination not to be an invalid.

'You lied to me,' she said slowly, her voice trembling with suppressed emotion. 'It was all a fraud.'

'It was for your own good. It wasn't a lie,' he protested, 'just an exaggeration. You and Gavin were meant for one another. You had no need to waste your energies on some poky little flat and a job you didn't need.'

Emily let out a shuddering breath; she'd wanted to be wrong. '*Your* good, you mean. I've heard this rumour that not all families are motivated by self-interest—just now I find the notion hard to believe.' Her expression hardened. She turned to Luke, who was watching the proceedings with undisguised interest. 'Get me out of here,' she commanded flatly. She had no intention of explaining the significance of the interchange. In one evening she had learnt that three of the people she had thought she knew best had all been deceiving her. Do I wear a label saying 'gullible idiot'? she wondered resentfully.

'I never thought you were a fool, until today.' Charles Stapely's expression was tight with contempt as he watched her lean into Luke's body as if the strength of his tall frame was all that prevented her from sliding to the ground. 'If you're that stupid, he's welcome to you. But if you suppose he's going to marry you, think again—'

'Actually, Father,' she interrupted, flushing slightly, 'we really haven't thought things out that far.' She acknowledged the troubled doubts that were stirring just on the edges of her consciousness, forced to wonder at the way she'd accepted Luke's ridiculous *fait accompli* with scant thought to the consequences of her actions.

'Thought!' Charles Stapely's fists bunched as he looked at Luke, who was eyeing the interchange from beneath half closed eyelids, very much at ease and not hiding his amusement at the proceedings. 'I doubt if you've thought at all; and just because you're in his bed, don't imagine you've got exclusive rights. He's just like his mother—not very discriminating… If it's breathing, bed it!'

Emily would have retreated if she could from the congealed loathing in her parent's voice. She was aware of the sudden tension in Luke's body. He was still standing directly behind her, an immovable barrier to her retreat.

'You're a pretentious, pompous fool,' Luke said almost casually. Emily, looking at his profile, could see a nerve throbbing erratically in his cheek. 'And if you ever so much as mention my mother again…' The threat was uttered in a pleasant voice that made it all the more sinister somehow. She saw her father recoil and fight to stand his ground when he looked into Luke's eyes.

'I've lived to regret ever taking you under my roof, you ingrate. And if you—' he pointed an accusing finger at

Emily '—if you go with him, you're no daughter of mine,' he told her in a voice shaking with rage. His parting, 'Wait till your mother hears about this,' was so petty after the grand gesture of disowning her that Emily found a gurgle of laughter escaping her throat.

She wiped her eyes, wondering whether her mascara was smeared across her face like warpaint. Looking at Luke, she was aware that for once she had surprised him.

'You don't sound too disturbed at being cast off,' he said, handing her a clean handkerchief.

'Just a touch of hysteria, that's all; besides, are my feelings actually of any interest to you? You *or* my father?' she asked, handing him back his handkerchief and giving him a straight look, her chin tilted at a defiant angle. They were both the same, she decided, each happy to use her to score points off the other. Manipulate whoever happened to be at hand.

'Keep it,' Luke advised. 'You might need it again before the night's over. Are you going to tell me precisely what that little scene was all about?'

'No.' She wasn't about to display her naïve credulity for his contempt. Besides, knowing Luke, he'd probably managed to get more than the bare bones of the incident. She waved away the handkerchief. 'Nowhere to put it,' she responded prosaically, then wished she hadn't because it drew Luke's glittering regard to her outfit. His eyes made her feel claustrophobic as they travelled at a leisurely pace over her slender but femininely curved—too curved for her own taste—body in the dress which covered too little of some of those curves.

'Quite true,' he agreed. His glance, returning to her face, held curiosity and something else she didn't care to analyse, although it made the pit of her stomach dissolve. 'I'll keep it for you.'

'I don't need anything of yours, and that goes for any smart moves like the one you pulled in there,' she ground out from between clenched teeth. If he thought he could divert her by doling out a dose of his particular brand of mesmeric sex appeal, he could think again. 'I can't believe you did it.' She shook her head. 'You just can't resist stirring, can you?' she accused hoarsely. The unmitigated nerve of the man, the undiluted arrogance, astonished her.

'I simply provided your inspiration. You were going to run away.'

'Sneer if you like, but running away is less painful at times. Besides, head-on collision doesn't always solve the problem.'

'Neither does running away; it just postpones the inevitable.'

'Thank you for that little gem,' she snapped. The accusation in his tone made her want to launch a frontal attack. 'At least my father was bright enough to disguise the fact that he was manipulating me. The only difference with you is I know it. Still, it's over with now.' She could retreat and let the wounds heal, sort out what she wanted from life.

'Oh, there are a lot more possibilities in this situation yet.'

Emily threw back her head, shaking her hair from around her shoulders. 'Forget it, Luke, I'm sick of the lot of you. I'm going to spend some time alone,' she told him, a flare of anger igniting dancing golden lights in her eyes. 'And I'm not available for any more theatricals, even if my stomach could stand up to being mauled about by you.'

'I don't think you've thought this out too clearly,' he said icily. He fixed his broad shoulders as if to ease some tension between his shoulder-blades.

'Of course I've not thought it out, you idiot,' she told him furiously. 'This is an emotional crisis, I'm devastated, hurt, my life is in ruins. Thinking,' she snarled, 'is not exactly easy at the moment. If it had been, I'd never have let you set up that little scene for your own sadistic purposes.'

'I expect you're not pleased at having all your plans upset. I mean, I'm sure this was one marriage where surprise was not on the menu,' he said with a faint sneer. 'You always did like your plans; I expect you'd timetabled the next twenty years. Your mistake was obviously telling pretty boy what he'd be doing with his life; he probably ran to your saintly sister in sheer panic.'

'You know nothing about it,' she snapped, her colour heightened. 'There's nothing wrong with organising—we don't all drift through life like some gypsy!'

He gave a deep laugh which she considered wildly inappropriate, and it only provided more proof of his total heartlessness, had such proof been necessary. 'Plans are made to have spanners aimed at them, infant, haven't you learnt that yet? Even if a man has slotted himself into a position which makes the rest of his life boringly inevitable, he doesn't need it spelt out for him. You probably had the progeny production timed with mathematical precision.'

'There's nothing indecent in a commitment,' she responded, stung by this unexpected assault. He made her sound as passionless as a computer! Gavin had never complained as she'd happily been involved in planning their future; she had been sure he'd wanted all the things she did. She gave a small sound of pain and bit her lip. Only he hadn't; that much was now painfully obvious.

'Why don't you admit it, Emmy? Your Gavin was just a convenient body who happened to meet your criteria at a time in your life you'd decided you should get married.'

The accusation took her breath away. 'I love Gavin,' she declared fiercely.

Luke looked unimpressed by her passionate declaration. 'Then perhaps you should have spent more time telling him so between the sheets and less organising him. Your only misjudgement was that the guy's got slightly more guts than you'd anticipated. You began moulding him a bit too early, sweetheart; you should have waited until after the wedding.'

She felt tears of fury sting her eyelids and she blinked furiously; she would not give him the satisfaction of seeing her cry. 'I hate you,' she said, not finding inspiration for a more original retort. But the worst part of it was that there was a grain of truth in what he said, and she wasn't blind enough to her own faults not to see it.

She liked and respected Gavin—at least she had; he was the only man she'd ever met whom she had considered spending her life with. She had been sure he would never bully her as her father did those around him. She had wondered whether the fact that her father was chairman of the bank and she his daughter had had anything to do with his assiduous courting.

'You can hardly go around saying that, infant, considering we are an…item,' Luke told her. His eyes watched the ripple of emotions running across her face, a sneer tugging at one corner of his mouth.

She made a sound of disgust in her throat. 'Don't get carried away with your fiction; that's over as of now. There was never any need to go as far as to molest me publicly,' she told him with a look of distaste. 'If you had bothered to consult me I could have told you so.'

'You prefer to be molested privately?' he said with polite interest. 'I could—'

'Keep your hands to yourself, Luke,' she cut in coldly. 'I don't find it amusing. I realise this is just a game to you, but it happens to be my life.' And a mess it was too.

'I take games very seriously,' he told her. 'For a planner you haven't looked beyond the next hour, have you?' he said, changing tack with bewildering abruptness.

Emily looked at him suspiciously. 'Should I?'

'Over and above the fact that your father has disowned

you, you seem to be overlooking our deep and abiding passion.'

He was laughing at her, she realised; if her mind hadn't been so confused, so cluttered with emotions, she would, she was sure, have understood what he was insinuating. 'Enlighten me,' she suggested testily.

'Our relationship can't fizzle out overnight.'

'Relationship? We haven't got a relationship,' she asserted, panic in her voice.

He continued as if she hadn't spoken. 'Or your stoical endurance of my passionate advances will have been in vain. Even stupid Charlotte will be able to see through the charade. It will be, Poor little Emily couldn't even hold her man. He preferred the sister, you know.'

'I'm not such a good liar as you so I'm afraid we might as well drop it,' she said, half relieved that the idea was folding almost before it had begun. One good thing had emerged: she was free from the guilt-induced bond that had held her a self-imposed prisoner at Charlcot.

'You underestimate my brilliance, infant.'

She closed her eyes and fantasised about wiping that irritatingly smug smile off his face. 'Don't call me that!'

'What, a term of endearment? And to think I thought you liked it.'

'You know I loathe it,' she contradicted him. 'That's why you do it.'

He gave her a sardonic look, his startling eyes as blue as a beneficent summer day and as sharp as jagged ice. 'Going back to my brilliance,' he said smoothly, and she wished fervently that she could penetrate that hateful composure.

Almost in flashback, a picture of him crouched with yells and smoke all around him, bullets singing through the air, recording the events going on around him economically but lucidly as if he weren't in danger of joining the reporter whose blood he was calmly staunching as he spoke, came

into her mind. That had been Luke's first time in front of
the camera rather than behind it, but not his last: the powers
that be hadn't needed the public response to the incident to
know a good thing when they saw it. After that Luke had
been seen reporting from various trouble-spots scattered
across the globe, but his first love had always been pho-
tography and he had never abandoned it.

It had been a job as a photographer on a daily newspaper
that Luke had taken in preference to the job her father had
offered him after university. When the opportunity had
arisen, he had accepted the challenge of moving to the live
medium, working for an independent new station. Her father, who had hated Luke's effortless progression, had
found his anonymity behind the lens easier to bear than the
public recognition that had come when he'd stepped to the
other side of the camera. She had seen him accept con-
gratulations of his famous relative with gritted teeth, knowing nothing would have pleased him more than if Luke had
failed miserably in every venture he began. He had hardly
been able to contain his fury when Luke had had a book
of his stills published; not content to concentrate on one
thing, he seemed to be able to shine in several skies at the
same time. The political thrillers which followed had
brought acclaim and monetary rewards as they'd lingered
indecently long in the bestseller lists. Her father had sim-
mered, and Emily had thought he had grown almost inured
to Luke's ability to juggle several careers and give the impression that he was only using a small portion of his talent.
She felt a mixture of envy and admiration, but at that moment she shared a portion of her parent's frustration. He
was so impervious, it made her want to stamp her feet!

'I think you're inhuman,' she announced.

'It's rather perverse of you to attack me...your saviour.'
He raised one eyebrow as she choked. 'And hardly a word
about pretty boy's infamy,' he remarked thoughtfully. 'As

I've been trying to tell you, I am going up to my cottage in Scotland to do some work on my book.'

'I didn't know you had a cottage in Scotland,' she said, surprised.

'Why should you?' he said in a tone that made her flush. 'You can come with me.'

'Thanks but no, thanks,' she retorted without thought.

'I can see the brain is overloaded again,' he said sympathetically. 'You can disappear with me for a decent interval and then reappear having seen me for what I am, or whatever story you care to invent. I favour the wild passion which burnt fiercely but briefly, but I leave the details to you.'

'You do surprise me,' she said, bristling. 'Do I actually have any say in the matter? I don't like being organised, in fact I hate it,' she hissed from between clenched teeth. She had absolutely no intention of going further than the end of the drive in Luke's company. He had extracted her from the immediate situation—she just needed time to think. One thing she didn't need—in fact the very thought made her feel a surge of undiluted panic—was to spend any more time with Luke.

'I know you prefer to do the organising, but look where that's landed you. Bossy women are not universally admired.'

She drew herself up to her full height and eyed him balefully. 'I'm so sorry I'm not a feminine, fluttery female,' she intoned sarcastically. 'You sexist pig! I take it it's all right for you to order me around? I'm supposed to be meekly submissive.'

'Meekly submissive is not the way I'd have described you, Emily,' he said drily. 'I was just trying to drop a hint or two. You're not exactly subtle, are you? And as for my suggestion, it was just that. I don't care whether you take me up on it,' he announced negligently, as though he was beginning to be bored by the whole conversation. 'It seemed the logical step to take, and if you can type or file you might even be useful,' he added thoughtfully.

Not if I can help it, she thought bitterly. 'You'll be able to torment Father for a little longer—I expect that's the main appeal.'

Luke gave a sudden grin, devilish lights reflected in his eyes. 'I gather you have a few reasons to be less than happy with Daddy, Em. The thought had occurred to me that Charlie will be tormented by images of sordid goings-on in the heather.'

Emily felt the colour seep beneath her skin, his words had conjured up an image so shocking and unexpected. Luke was staring at her, his expression broodingly speculative. She registered the dark shadows beneath his eyes and the shadow of stubble that covered his cheeks and jaw. It gave him an air of attractive dissipation, although she knew it probably just indicated incipient exhaustion. Luke kept himself in superb condition; he couldn't survive at the pace he set himself if he didn't exhibit some self-control. She was thinking along the lines of exercise and diet... Women, that was another matter. Did her cousin usually take women up to his Scottish retreat? If he did, did he expect...? Her eyes opened wide in sudden sharp alarm.

'Are you actually suggesting that we—?' She broke off, searching for the correct terminology to cover this problem.

'I'm anxious to inflict some mental anguish of a severe degree on your family, Emily, but I'm not willing to exert myself that much, infant.'

The swing of her arm was pure reflex. She registered the darkening mark along his cheek, wondering if he would retaliate. He appeared quite unmoved by her tears and she was furious with her uncontrollable response.

'You always were a bully.'

'And you were always a pampered brat,' he replied dispassionately. She froze when he grasped her chin, forcing her to look up into his eyes. 'You were always trying to get attention, I seem to recall.'

She tried to jerk away, a hot denial on her lips.

'You have a very selective memory, infant. Oh, I quite forgot, you're a mature woman these days,' he drawled mockingly. 'Strange, I doubt that—despite outer appearances.' His unoccupied hand rose to trace carelessly the outline of her breast from the fabric-covered under-curve to the bare upper slope.

The casual intimacy induced an instantaneous physical response of her flesh, which she endured with confused misery. She swallowed a constriction in her dry throat, aware of the rasp of fabric against her sensitised flesh. The bodice of her dress seemed suddenly painfully tight.

'The sort of attentions you gave me were delightful interludes. Like throwing me in the lake in November.' She breathed deeply, regaining a little equilibrium now that his hand was no longer in contact with her flesh, even though his cool fingers seemed to have left an imprint like a brand on her skin. 'Or pushing my face in the dirt,' she added, warming to her theme. 'And—'

'All of which were preferable to indifference.'

He must have seen the dawning of awareness flicker in her eyes.

'Y-you were incredibly awful to me,' she faltered.

'I believe the punishment usually fitted the crime.'

'Children may have few rights to speak of,' she replied, barely coping with an odd breathlessness that was afflicting her, 'but I'm an independent agent now. And I have no intention of going anywhere with you except away from the immediate precincts of Charlcot.'

'How long before you're back?' he sneered. 'Living at home at twenty has to limit your emotional development to some extent, even when the said home has all the anonymity of a hotel.' He gave her a look of mild contempt.

'A five-star hotel, of course. No wonder you still act like a spoilt brat.'

'The way I live my life has got nothing to do with you.'

'Live?' he drawled sarcastically.

'I would have left home,' she began, stung by the contempt. It was easy for him—nothing had ever been there to hold him back. She envied his freedom. I'm free now, she reminded herself: no fiancé, no terminally ill father to be mollified. Should I be celebrating? A bubble of hysteria rose in her throat.

Luke was watching her closely…was that concern? No, it couldn't be, she decided. 'Emily…' He spoke her name angrily, with an urgency that made the wild laughter die abruptly.

'So it's true.' Her mother's strident voice broke the brief strained silence.

Emily sighed, feeling suddenly weary. She hadn't heard her father bring in reinforcements. Here we go again! she thought. As if he'd picked up the energy draining from her, Luke interposed himself between her mother and herself. Not out of any wish to preserve her sanity, she thought, assailed by a strange nebulous hunger. More likely he didn't want her to end the farce before he had extracted all the spiteful revenge he possibly could from the situation.

Her mother was as cold as her father had been hot; the gist of her words indicated that she wasn't surprised at Emily's behaviour. Emily listened to her whole life being described as a deliberate series of actions geared to give her parents the utmost degree of distress. She had the impression that her mother felt somehow vindicated by this final example of her ungrateful behaviour.

She stood frozenly dazed as her mother swept out of the room, dismissing her youngest child, her thoughts concentrated only on minimising the scandal attached to an engagement broken almost before it had been born.

'Such warmth, such compassion,' she heard Luke mur-

mur. She looked at him, surprise widening her blank eyes as he draped his jacket across her shoulders. It held the soothing heat of his body. She gave an involuntary shudder.

His face was lacking the usual mockery as he met her cautious look. She nibbled her lower lip in quiet agitation. The involuntary action attracted his attention, his eyes sliding towards her, his mouth narrowed.

'It's not over yet,' he said abruptly, 'so don't fall apart.'

Emily swallowed and lowered her eyes, feeling a ridiculous anticlimax. Had she actually been holding her breath waiting for compassion, understanding? I must be losing my mind, she remonstrated with herself derisively. She didn't need that sort of support. She'd seen her parents' unconcern turn Charlotte into a creature pathetically eager to please, filled with a need to have a stronger person to cling to in times of stress. This had led her to lean heavily on Emily herself and a string of wildly unsuitable men, all of whom had in common a very high regard for themselves, which Charlotte had mistakenly assumed was strength. Emily, on the other hand, had deliberately avoided the trap of turning to casual relationships for solace; instead she'd become self-sufficient and unapologetically proud of her lack of dependence.

She shrugged off his jacket, her bones protesting as the cold replaced the soothing heat. All kindnesses from Luke should be greeted with suspicion—she'd almost forgotten this cardinal rule; he was passionate only in his need to inflict retribution. She didn't know the details of what her parents had done to earn his life-long enmity, and she had never delved into the family closet, seeing no point in rattling skeletons. But if he did have any gentler feelings they would never be wasted on a Stapely.

She recalled his bizarre accusation earlier; in some way he held her father personally responsible for his own mother's death, and a shiver crept up the length of her spine. There was a dark side to Luke, and she didn't want to see it.

'I'm not going to fall apart,' she told him with a quiet dignity. He accepted the garment she held out, a smile twisting his lips. 'Could you wait in the car? I want to speak to Gavin alone, and collect a few things,' she said with a prosaic practicality she was far from feeling. 'You can take me to a hotel.'

'I'll give you thirty minutes and then I'll come and get you.'

She accepted this ultimatum with an angry look, but didn't bite back with the childish retort that hovered on her tongue.

CHAPTER THREE

'WE'LL STAY AT my place tonight.'

Emily nodded, without noticing the discreetly satisfied smile of victory that curved Luke's mouth as he drove the low-slung, powerful car along the narrow country lanes. She couldn't even summon up enough interest to wonder much about the pillow she would lay her head on. She would find a hotel tomorrow—it was late.

She sat with her back rigidly in contact with the upholstered seat, her body unable to accept the luxury and relax. She couldn't stop reliving the inevitable interview with Gavin. It had been like talking to a stranger, not the man she had planned up to a few hours ago to spend the rest of her life with. Why was I going to marry him? she found herself wondering. Could her motivation really be as shallow and unemotional as Luke suggested? She couldn't, wouldn't believe that.

Gavin's response to her confession had been mixed. She had seen the small flash of relief as he'd assimilated her words—so small, that, if she hadn't been expecting it, steeling herself for it, she might have missed it. More surprising had been the anger, the pique. It had stilled the apology she had been going to make herself utter, to add to the reality of the affair before it had been born. His hypocrisy had been worse in some way than his betrayal. She could see that, even while he was glad of his painless escape, he was angry that she had had the temerity to be the one to admit seeking solace elsewhere.

Listening to him express his disappointment, his pain, she had almost forgotten that she was innocent and he was the one who had cheated. She had bitten her lip till blood tasted salty on her tongue to stop her angry, astringent response. His, his, his—did he care about anyone else? Herself, Charlotte? His handsome face had had such a sanctimonious expression that she'd wanted to fling the truth in his face, turn her retreat into an attack, but she had her pride. Better by far to be the one to pull the curtain over the episode.

'Did you see Charlotte?'

Pulled back to the present, she glanced at Luke's averted profile. The eyes of a startled night animal scuttling across the road caught the headlights, and he reacted automatically, slowing the pace to allow the night creature to escape.

'I decided not to.' That was the one person she hadn't been able to face; the mingled emotions of anger and, amazingly, compassion were too intricately mingled. She couldn't trust her reactions; she might well have blurted out the truth in her present chaotic state of mind. She couldn't accept the pain her sister had knowingly inflicted upon her.

'How will you feel if Gavin marries her?'

'Don't skirt around the issue, as if you're worried about my feelings; just get straight to the point,' she responded with tight-lipped irony, her brown eyes suffused with outrage at this insensitive question. 'I expect you hover around accidents waiting for the ambulance, revelling in all that pain and gore.'

'Society does have a certain morbid fascination with disaster,' he agreed calmly. 'I expect I'm as guilty as most; it's difficult to know where empathy ends and thrill-seeking begins. But in this case there can be no cause for error. I have no sympathy for you, Emily; in fact I think it's fortunate that fate has stepped in to stop you living out the cosy little family fantasy you've constructed.'

She caught her breath and counted very slowly to ten. 'How silly of me. Until you pointed it out I hadn't quite appreciated my good fortune.'

'Any time,' he said, throwing a provoking grin over his shoulder before pulling out on to the dual carriageway.

Emily didn't trust herself to speak—his smugness was almost intolerable. Sleep crept over her swiftly and she wasn't conscious of Luke stopping the car and easing her limp body into a more comfortable position.

She hovered in the grey area between consciousness and repose, unwilling to make the transition. A loud roar and a sudden flash of lights snapped her awake. 'What...?'

'Motorbikes heading for the local orthopaedic ward, if I'm not mistaken.'

Emily stifled a yawn and stretched her limbs, stiff from being too long in one position. She looked out of the window. The motorway was anonymous and surprisingly quiet. 'Have I been asleep long?' She felt appalling—dry, stale mouth and incipient throbbing headache.

'Four hours.'

She stiffened, and her eyes swivelled in the direction she'd so far avoided. Luke didn't take his eyes from the clear stretch of carriageway in front of him. 'Pardon?' She quelled the spasm of panic—she must have misheard him. From Charlcot to Luke's warehouse conversion in London would have taken an hour and a half, and that estimate was generous.

'Four hours, Emily, accompanied by the sweet music of your snores.'

'I don't snore,' she responded automatically.

'Is that what Gavin told you, infant?'

Emily frowned and threw off the last remnants of sleep. She wasn't in the mood to be side-tracked. 'You said four hours.'

'This conversation is taking a somewhat circular route, Emmy. I don't expect sparkling wit, but—'

'Don't try being smart with me,' she snapped. 'Where the hell are we? We're not going to your flat.'

He shot her a sideways glance of infuriating complacence. 'I didn't say we were.'

She felt the heat travel up her neck and spill into her cheeks. If he hadn't been driving, she'd have…'You *did*,' she contradicted from between clamped teeth. 'Spend the night at your place, your London flat, you said. Where are you taking me?' she demanded.

'My place,' he agreed blandly. 'I didn't specify *which* place. I hate to sound boastful, but I have a farmhouse in Tuscany, no running water and a view to die for—'

'I wish you would,' she snarled.

He clicked his tongue. 'As I was saying, the place in Tuscany, a modest but upwardly mobile apartment in New York, and my Scottish retreat.'

'I don't believe you.' He wasn't doing this! She stared at him with wild-eyed horror; not even Luke would pull a stunt like this.

He threw her a look of injured innocence. 'Would I lie?'

'You're taking me to Scotland.'

'Would you have preferred New York?' he asked with a note of sympathy. 'Maybe one day, if you mend your manners.'

She let out a groan of sheer frustration and rage. 'I'd prefer you to stop this car instantly!'

He winced and rubbed his ear. 'The word fishwife immediately springs to mind.'

'The words dangerous lunatic follow closely.'

He laughed then, sounding so relaxed and at ease that only a sense of self-preservation stopped her hitting out at him physically. A car smash would be the end to a perfect day!

'Aren't you over-reacting just a mite?' he observed, moving into the outside lane to overtake a monstrous articulated lorry.

'Over-reacting?' she squeaked. 'I can see it's most un-reasonable of me, but I tend to get overwrought...'

'And emotional...'

She examined his perfect profile with loathing. '...And emotional,' she agreed with irony, 'when kidnapped.'

'A strong word,' he said in a tone which still suggested he was treating the whole affair with a flippancy that made her want to scream.

'An accurate word.'

'I said my place and you made no protests,' he reminded her.

'Your place being London, not some god-forsaken spot north of the border. I made it perfectly clear that I had no intention of going to Scotland.'

'You don't care for the country?'

'I don't care for you.' For a split-second his eyes met hers; the intensity of the colour of the iris was always a surprise. The expression that flickered into the dense, drowning blue was elusive but violently intense. It washed over her like some insidious drug and the words of protest stilled in her throat. 'Keep your eyes on the road,' she managed hoarsely. She endured another few excruciating seconds before he obliged her. She slumped back in the seat feeling drained and furious.

'This is absurd, Luke.' She tried to inject a note of sanity into the proceedings. 'It's generally considered unacceptable to hijack a person.'

'I was going to Scotland. I saw no reason to alter my plans for you, infant.'

'I wasn't asking you to; I didn't ask you to interfere.'

A grim smile curved his lips. 'It was a pleasure,' he asserted obliquely, leaving her to wonder whether the pleasure he had discovered had been in infuriating her father or the liberties he had taken with herself.

'I won't go with you.'

'You *are* with me,' he pointed out patiently.

His attitude made her feel as if she was hitting her head against a particularly solid wall. 'Have you no conscience? You've kidnapped me! It's uncivilised,' she choked.

The glance he flicked her was brief and starkly savage. 'I'm sorry if you find my methods crude...often they are the most effective. Being civilised can be damnably time-consuming,' he observed.

One look at his profile made it obvious that she was wasting her time. With a sound of frustration, tears flooding her eyes, she gripped the door-handle and rattled it.

'Seventy miles an hour and she decides to make a leap for freedom.' The eyebrows shot heavenwards. 'Smooth move, Emmy. Just thank your stars for central locking.'

'This is criminal. I'll have you arrested,' she threatened him wildly. She brushed her hand over her face, blotting the stray spots of dampness where her eyes had overflowed. 'I'll tell my father,' she added miserably.

'I'm relying on it.'

Emily shot him a startled glance. 'So that's what this is all about,' she said flatly. 'You're prepared to go to a lot of trouble just to needle my father.'

'Needle?' he said, not bothering to deny her accusation. 'I think you underestimate your importance, infant. You're his ewe lamb,' he sneered. 'The apple of his eye. The prospect of you sharing my humble abode and all it implies should have a most satisfactory effect.'

'So glad I could be of use,' she said witheringly. 'I don't suppose my feelings enter into your machinations?'

'I think the change of scene should do you good.'

'Give me strength!' she groaned. 'I've had a gut full of people knowing what my best interests are; roughly translated, it means I'm supposed to do what I'm told. Well, you might be able to get me to your hovel but don't expect me to stay. The first opportunity I have I'll be off, and I'll report you to the authorities.'

'I'll keep that in mind, Emily,' he replied gravely.

Rat! she fumed. He'd smirk on the other side of his face. He'd find she could be a very unpleasant house guest.

'Music?' he asked as she maintained a fulminating silence.

She pursed her lips and shrugged. The strains of Debussy failed to soothe her intense fury. The feelings of impotence to resolve the situation made her want to rant and scream, but she wasn't going to give him the pleasure of seeing how far he'd actually shaken her. Isolation and Luke were a combination she instinctively knew she should avoid.

He only stopped once during the rest of the journey and that was only when she explained the urgency of the request. He still looked remarkably alert considering how far he had driven on top, if he was to be believed, of a plane journey. She felt as spent as a limp rag, emotionally and physically.

'Ullapool,' he said as they passed through a small village that nestled picturesquely on the shores of Loch Broom. 'You can see the Russian fishing fleet out there—' he gestured seawards '—when the mist clears.'

'It isn't permanent, then,' she returned with a sarcastic drawl.

They'd driven through the night and the hazy morning light revealed a damp landscape covered in a thick, obscuring cloud of mist. Mountains loomed threateningly indistinct, dark, monstrous shapes, and the sea was a sound, an expanse of emptiness. Used to tame, governable, neatly hedged fields, she sensed that there was an empty canvas which was just veiled, and found it awesome.

'Wait and see.'

'I won't be staying long enough,' she retorted. 'Is it far? I'm tired.' She felt bone-weary, the toll of the past hours beginning to tell with a vengeance.

'Twenty-five miles. So if you thought Ullapool was the back of beyond, think again,' he advised.

She was almost grateful that the weather conditions and

the single track road that hugged some precipitous drops at times eliminated the need for her to think up any defensive replies. Luke needed all his concentration for the task of getting them safely to their destination. Emily, who at times felt inclined to shriek as they encountered yet another tortuous bend, was impressed by his calm handling of the big car.

EMILY STARED around the large, sparsely furnished kitchen. A large stone ingle-nook took up an entire wall. A cast-iron wood-burner nestled comfortably in its centre, a pile of chopped logs conveniently stacked to one side.

To her amazement there were all the modern conveniences, neatly disguised for the most part by doors that matched the rustic pine kitchen units. The beamed roof was low, but the light Mediterranean colours made the place seem light, airy and welcoming.

'It's very nice,' she said, her voice reflecting amazement.

Luke dumped the bags he'd carried in on the long refectory table. 'What had you anticipated, no electricity or running water?' He looked at her face. 'O thou of little faith; as if I'd expose a delicate little flower like yourself to such indignities.'

The delicate flower swung a wild punch which he side-stepped. 'Next you'll be expecting me to thank you.'

'Thanks from a Stapely? Hardly. In the meantime, help me fetch the things in.'

She watched him pick up the envelope propped in the centre of the table and open it. His eyes scanned the contents. 'Fetch your own things in,' she retorted petulantly. As always, the way he said her name gave the impression that it left a nasty taste in his mouth. She'd seen his name inscribed in capitals on the envelope, probably perfumed paper, she thought scornfully, assuming instantaneously that the author of the missive was female.

His eyes darkened as he tucked the note in his trouser

pocket. 'If you want your stuff, get it, Miss Stapely. I'm not your lackey. And if you're going to explore, be careful; this is the only habitable room down here. I'm renovating it room by room and some of the floors are hazardous,' he informed her.

'I want to go home, Luke,' she said, the plaintive winning out over the aggressive in her quavering voice.

He placed the last of his burdens on the flagged floor and shut the heavy oak studded door. A door built to keep out the most severe of elements. His eyes swept over her slight figure thoughtfully. 'I'll light the fire,' he said as she shivered, her arms clamped around herself to retain heat. He moved over to the ingle-nook. 'Matches in the bottom drawer of the dresser.'

The imperious way he held out his hand, apparently certain that she would jump, refuelled her sense of injustice. 'I told you I want to go home,' she repeated. The high-handed way he'd coerced her into being here was still almost impossible to take in. The fact that she was almost incidental in the exercise was an added insult; just an instrument to twist the knife in her father's flesh...it was disgusting!

'I thought you'd been cast off, a homeless stray,' he murmured with his back still to her. He stayed crouched beside the fire and rolled up his sleeves. Her eyes, with a will of their own, were drawn to his forearms; the fine sprinkling of dark hairs was in danger, she realised furiously, of making her stare like some witless idiot. 'Or was that just a cosmetic exercise? Had you planned to go back in a couple of days and be Daddy's good little girl? I'm sure even Gavin will seem acceptable once he's seen the error of his ways.' He turned his head, his blue eyes glittering with contempt.

His derision cut through her bewildering fascination with certain mundane details of his person. 'I'd sooner marry—' Her eyes glittered and her chest heaved as she searched for

the worst fate she could imagine '—you than Gavin.' Her
brief feeling of triumph faded as she encountered the very
disturbing expression that flickered into his eyes.

'That would be something to write home about, wouldn't
it, sweetheart?' His smile was subtly sensuous. 'Was that
a proposal?'

'Don't be stupid,' she snapped, unbalanced by his response. 'Where are the matches?' she said, more to divert
him than to be a willing little helper. The gleam of ironic
laughter in his eyes made it abundantly clear that her tactics, like her unease, were as easy for him to read as foot-
high type.

'Bottom drawer of the dresser,' he said after holding her
defiant gaze for a moment. 'Thank you.' Unnecessarily he
caught hold of her hand as he took the box, his thumb
moving over the blue-veined inner aspect of her wrist.

Her wide, startled eyes were captured by his for a split-
second before she snatched her hand away. Neat electricity
travelled to her toes. Contact gone, the current was broken—but not the unpleasant after-effects. She sat in a high-
backed Windsor chair, her knees feeling incapable of supporting her at that moment.

'Why exactly do you hate us so much?'

There was a hiss and the kindling caught fire. His eyes
were gem-hard when he turned. With the elegance that was
such an integral part of him he straightened up. 'Us?'

She took a deep breath; the taboo subject had been
broached and she intended to get to the bottom of it. She
was no longer a child to have her questions smiled away.
'You know exactly what I mean,' she said impatiently.
'What particular sin have the Stapelys committed?' It had
puzzled her half her lifetime. It was no normal antipathy
he felt, something much more complex. Beneath his casual
contempt there was always something which eluded her.

'Are you trying to tell me you don't know?' His voice
was tinged with incredulous scorn.

'I know your mother was disowned by her adoptive mother, and she ran off because…' She felt suddenly embarrassed at cold-bloodedly discussing Luke's history as though the people involved were characters in a novel as opposed to people with feelings. Did her curiosity sound crude and clumsy? But she was suddenly sure that it was relevant to the present, and she had conceived a strong, dog-like tenacity to get to the bones at long last.

'She was pregnant with me,' Luke supplied, his lips forming into a cynical smile. 'Hackneyed but accurate. There's no need to get all coy—I can recall several occasions when you flung that fact at me in moments of pique.'

Emily took a deep breath, a swift, horrified denial springing to her lips. 'I…' Mortified, she realised his accusation was unpalatably true. She had been a little brat at times.

'My mother supported us both until I was ten. I won't bore you with the details of a life which by your standards would have seemed impoverished,' he drawled. 'She found out at that point that she had a disease which was likely to leave me an orphan prematurely.'

Emily found herself straining to listen to his unemotional narrative. Her eyes grew dark at the dilemma which had faced this unknown woman, and part of her wondered whether she who had never had to face such harsh realities could have coped even up to that point, bringing up a child alone. She felt a surge of inadequacy when faced with such self-sacrifice.

'So she swallowed her pride and decided to turn to her family. The old lady was long dead and lacking any direct heir—at least one she would recognise. She had left the lot to your father, her nephew, with the proviso that he would take responsibility for her grandchild in the event of my mother's demise. Charlie pointed out that my mother had not at that point died.' He raised his eyes to her horror-struck face, and his expression was inflexibly hard, as

though his features were hewn out of marble rather than
flesh and blood. It was at that moment she realised the
depth of his hatred, his rage.

The realisation was a profound experience. Luke's contempt, his casual derision, all took on a new dimension.
Had she been stupid not to look below the surface before?
The question swirled together with a multitude of others in
the chaotic morass of speculation that shook her to the
foundations...challenged all the parameters of her life.

'I won't go into the details of just how much she suffered,' he said, his voice aloof, only his eyes alive with an
active fury that added momentum to the warning bells of
disquiet in her head. 'She was a tough woman, but I
watched her grow weaker, frailer. I was impotent to help.
Shall we just say I made a vow a long time ago to admin-
ister a suitable punishment?'

'You were a child,' she protested huskily.

'Childhood is a modern concept. Children are capable of
great passion just as some adults are capable of insipid
apathy.' He looked at her, contempt twisting his expression.

She couldn't doubt that his comment was intended to be
personal, but she was too preoccupied by his revelations to
react to the fact. 'Are you using me?' Crazy ideas that her
present situation had been contrived for his own malignant
purpose refused to retreat, even though logic told her the
suspicion was misplaced. If the tender scene in the conservatory had been a shock to her, there couldn't have been
any way for Luke to have predicted it. No, he had just taken
the heaven-sent opportunity it presented to him to inflict as
much pain on the Stapelys as possible, and she had been
almost co-operative from his point of view...stupid from
her own.

Luke's eyes were blatantly mocking. 'I thought we'd already agreed that this was a mutually beneficial arrangement. You knew you were a contrivance, so why the wide-
eyed horror now?' he drawled.

'I have agreed to nothing; I've been coerced. Besides, that was before...' she began falteringly. What he'd said was true, but then it hadn't had the same significance. She hadn't been prepared for the depth, the shocking intensity, of his revulsion. His attitude had always seemed to spring from a certain perverse desire to challenge her parents' blinkered, smug outlook on life, but this dark hatred that had taken seed all those years ago was quite different. It had been there all along beneath the urbane exterior, a core of lethal ire, a passion that craved justice. She wasn't at all sure any more, looking at a face stripped bare of all languid cynicism, just how far he was prepared to go in his crusade. She shivered, suddenly aware of the cold in the room that seemed to seep from the stone walls. The isolation was like an emptiness in the pit of her stomach.

'Before you caught a glimpse of the real world?'

'None of this seems very real to me,' she said, her voice filled with the weariness that made her droop quite literally with lassitude. 'I didn't ask to be spirited away here; in fact, I specifically told you I wouldn't come. You haven't listened to a word I've said from the outset. What is it with you? The gospel according to Saint Luke?' She shook her head. 'Why can't you let the past die?'

'Like my mother?'

'You said before that my father killed your mother. But she took her own life, Luke.' She felt no urge, especially at the moment to defend her father, but the injustice of that accusation still bothered her.

'She couldn't provide for me any longer,' he replied in a cold, clipped voice. 'Charlie had made it pretty clear that he was only going to honour his obligations to the letter. A little light on morality, Charlie, isn't he?' he said, watching her pale face with narrow-eyed implacability. 'Can you imagine the desperation that made her step out under that bus? She did it for me, Emmy, so that I could have a home, food, safety—all the things you, sweetheart, have taken for granted all your life.'

She raised her dark-rimmed eyes to his face in startled enquiry. 'Is that why you've decided to ruin my life?' she flung.

He caught the back of a chair, his knuckles white against the dark wood. It made a discordant sound on the stone-flagged floor. 'Melodramatic, don't you think? Especially when all I've done is be incredibly helpful and get lumbered with a sulky neurotic who expects to be waited on hand and foot.'

'What? Is this a case of the sins of the fathers?' she snapped back, her throat aching with the sheer injustice of his casual accusations. 'I wish I'd never allowed you to persuade me to take part in this farce originally!' If she'd known from the outset how far he was prepared to go, she'd have known better than to take his offer of help. How could I have been so stupid? she wondered incredulously.

'About time you decided to take responsibility for your own actions, Emily. You were eager enough to preserve your precious pride, as I recall. It didn't take any persuasion on my part. You always seem willing to take the easy way out.'

At that moment she knew it would be easier to face the indignity of being jilted than endure another second of Luke's company. 'Wasn't that what your mother was doing—paying for the consequences of her own actions? Or is it the money that bothers you? Dad getting the money that should have gone to you.' His fingers dug into her forearms, cutting through to the bone, stilling the impetuous words that had emerged in her desire to challenge his scalding scorn.

She hadn't for an instant meant her acid remarks. In fact the knowledge that her own father was capable of such cold-blooded, corrupt behaviour made her want to weep. Her attack had been more defensive, but her choice of weapons ill-considered. But she wanted desperately to hurt him as much as he had her. To be nothing but a pawn to be manoeuvred by two manipulative men was mortifying.

'The idea of the sins of the father being visited on your head is a concept growing in attractiveness by the instant,' he said grimly. The look of rage in his eyes made her grow defiantly rigid; even though his fingers were making her nerve-endings scream in pain, she would die rather than let him see how truly frightened she was in that instant. 'You are his favourite. As much as Charlie,' he drawled the name with distaste, '*can* care about anyone, he cares for you, the baby of the family, cosseted, indulged.'

Confined, stifled, given objects, not love, she wanted to add. 'I can appreciate continuity,' she said instead, her voice shaking with emotion. 'After all, your mother's sins visited on you; why not blame her?'

'You little bitch,' he said slowly. 'You have fewer scruples than I gave you credit for. In some people's eyes it might be considered more a sin to select a breeding line cold-bloodedly than to give yourself without reservation in a moment of supreme passion, giving without a guarantee of anything. But then, you Stapelys think a lot of breeding lines and pedigrees, don't you? My mother only fulfilled expectations—but what can you expect of a stray who can't trace its ancestors back to William the Conqueror?'

She felt dizzy, unable to look away from the contemptuous azure gaze. His initial accusation made her instinctively want to scream denial. It hadn't been like that with Gavin. Perhaps she hadn't felt the blind love that she'd heard such a lot about, but the fact was that she'd given up waiting for a bolt from the blue to strike her. Once she'd nursed the usual fantasies, but they'd stayed just that. The self-inflicted suffering which followed the trauma of an infatuation at the tender age of sixteen had made her distrust her own instincts, shy away from emotional experimentation.

Eventually she had accepted the incident as a one-off. Either she wasn't capable of grand passion or the emotion had been exaggerated beyond all recognition by a kind of mass wishful thinking.

'I think you're talking about sex,' she sneered. Pulling her actions apart pragmatically, she could see that to some Luke's accusations might seem almost justified. What was wrong with friendship, common interest and compatibility as reasons for marriage? It had to be more lasting than a brief chemical explosion—that made for temporary insanity.

'Never the twain shall meet, hey, Emmy?' A sudden mellowness, a huskiness that was caressingly smooth, had entered his voice, and the transition from steely wrath was disorientating.

Staring up at him, she was aware of a heaviness in her eyelids, an urgent desire to melt quietly into the golden grip of lassitude that swept over her like ripples on a still lake, growing in urgency. 'Next you'll be telling me you're a romantic,' she retorted, fighting the drowning sensation. She could see her own features exaggerated like a caricature in his eyes—strangely hypnotic eyes.

Luke's eyes were travelling over her face with an almost reluctant intensity, as if he was submitting to a need he rejected and resented. His gaze rested on a spot on her throat where a pulse visibly beat with erratic force.

'Don't!' The panic-stricken word emerged strangled from between her trembling lips. She didn't know what was happening to her; she felt powerless to combat the drowning sensation. She felt intensely conscious of her own body, of the way her pulse was racing, the tenderness in her breasts as they brushed against her shirt, the growing ache low in her belly and a vague, mingled confusion of fear and impatience.

A growl was torn from his throat before his mouth covered hers. The movement was hard, hungry; she absorbed the impression of warmth, fragrant moisture, a sensation of overwhelming intimacy that made her body grow soft and pliant, her senses tuned to the tumultuous response that was building up within her.

With a sudden cry, lost in his mouth, her arms went around his waist; unable to meet across the expanse of his back, her fingers dug into the hardly muscled expanse as, with a series of small whimpers, she plastered herself against him.

Being removed physically from him was such a shock that it was several seconds before the sense of intense deprivation would permit her chest to expand sufficiently to breathe. Humiliation didn't take long to supplant the insidious hunger that had conspired to sweep away her better judgement. She was overwhelmed by the appalling weakness that had made her a willing—no, eager—participant.

She had thought she could handle this awareness, an awareness of the aggressive sensuality that Luke simply oozed and her own reluctant acknowledgement that she was responding to it at any number of inappropriate moments. But this! She inwardly cringed at the eager way she had co-operated with the somewhat brutal onslaught. He hadn't even tried to seduce her tenderly, she realised, and it had been *he* who had halted the escalation; that was the crowning humiliation.

Her chest rising with the exertion of combating the sensations that were quietly dragging her apart, she met his eyes, and stared at the person she held directly responsible for the violation of her will.

'I believe you mentioned something about sex,' he drawled slowly as she chewed her lower lip, her expression defiant but apprehensive, the flesh along her high cheekbones still tinged with a delicate colour all the more apparent because of the pallor of the rest of her face. 'Not a very refined performance, but I believe you got the drift.'

The cool, analytical expression on his face made something deep inside her rebel. How could she have revealed so much of herself when so little had been offered? she wondered despairingly. It was becoming clearer by the second. It had been a major error of judgement being here when, short of sprouting wings, she had to endure Luke's company. Not that she had had much say in the matter!

'Why did you do that?' she asked, her voice accusing, trembling.

He shrugged. 'You wanted me to,' he announced casually, and his lips thinned in an expression of almost bored scorn as she swelled with angry denial. 'You don't imagine I'd actually *choose* to kiss your father's daughter, do you?' he asked disparagingly, pushing the chair beside him with a jerky, violent movement that made it crash to the floor with a noise they both ignored. 'You always were an insidious little thing,' he said, speaking oddly, the words swift and angry. 'Big eyes that managed to look as though I'd inflicted some mortal wound. Those eyes managed to make a person forget you were the little girl who had everything, including an in-built sense of superiority, a deep conviction that everything would fall into your lap without you raising a finger. If it didn't, Daddy would fix it. Is that why it hurt so much to find out Gavin had been cheating, Em? Couldn't you believe anyone would dare not to fit in with your scheme?'

A faint frown marred her brow as she glared at him. The rush of angry contempt was bewilderingly swift. She didn't even bother formulating a defence; her childhood had been less than blissful, and if she had felt some odd affinity with Luke it had probably been because he was the only person who had ever treated her as though she wasn't some human equivalent of fast food—to provide instant gratification on the occasions a little girl was meant to be displayed, and ignored in the interim.

Something didn't quite add up. For a moment there he had seemed just as eager a participant as she had...the next he was behaving as though she made his skin crawl. Could men fake things so completely? she wondered miserably, flushing as she recalled the hard arousal of his body pressed against her own. 'If you touch me again I'll…I'll make you sorry,' she flung at him hotly.

'Perhaps I just wanted to mess up your pragmatic little mind. Sex can do that.' He gave a low, mocking laugh. 'The word makes you blush virginally. Did Gavin like the *ingénue* approach? Do you always light up at the flick of a switch?' he continued on a note of curiosity. 'I don't know why you're quite this mad, infant, or do you save the fireworks for the ones with serious intentions?'

'If my ancestry troubles you so much, I don't really see why my sexuality or lack of it need concern you at all,' she snapped back, unhappy by his casual reference to her instantaneous reaction to him. Silently she cursed fate that she was so susceptible to the one man on the face of the earth who definitely wasn't for her. She'd found out what she'd been missing, and she wished she hadn't.

'All alone in the middle of nowhere,' he said reflectively. 'A man might forget his qualms and take advantage of his opportunity…' He let his voice trail away, his expression terrifyingly speculative.

Emily was sure it was bluff, but all the same… She recalled his expression of fastidious distaste a little earlier, when he had derided the idea of actually making love to her from anything other than a desire to humiliate, exact punishment for the accident of her birth… He wouldn't go that far to exact revenge, would he? Alarm and uncertainty swept through her veins. She looked at him through the veil of her long lashes—his intolerable complacency made her want to scream.

He was no better than her father, for all his faults. No, he was worse, she decided, recalling the bewitching touch of his hands lightly touching her body… Heavens, he'd been able to turn her into a quivering wreck without even touching her, she thought on a rising tide of despair.

'Am I supposed to be terrified?' she enquired with a calm interest that was at odds with the curious sensation she felt, akin to the mingled fear and exhilaration experienced when a big dipper had reached the peak of its ascent and goose-bumps rose under the skin. 'Because, if so, save it,' she advised tartly. 'After all, you might to able to fool the masses who are blessed enough not to know you, but I do and I've never liked you,' she told him in a quivering voice. 'So snide, so bloody superior! Of course, my father's despicable—I'm no idiot, I can accept that. But he *is* my father. You look down from your morally superior heights and with the same breath calmly manipulate people to further your own ends. You're no better than he is!' At this point it behoved her to make a sweeping exit, but after one step she realised that there *was* no exit. She stopped uncertainly in the middle of the room, feeling inexplicably foolish under his steely stare.

The silence in the room was oppressive. Emily wondered whether he was going to let her fling those accusations with impunity.

'Did Gavin know about the temper?' he said half to himself with a penetrating appraisal from his sapphire eyes before a slow, devastating smile relieved the grimness of his expression. 'Perhaps that was why he felt obliged to agree with you, infant, for fear of the sharp edge of your tongue.'

'Gavin never did anything...' she began before she recalled exactly what Gavin had done.

'Except sleep with the sister?' He shrugged. 'But it's all in the family, isn't it? I find it strange that you react so much more violently to my relatively minor misdemeanour. After all, a few home truths and a kiss or two wouldn't rate on most folks' scale of unacceptable behaviour as equal to sleeping with the fiancée's sister.' His eyes narrowed and his thumbs hooked in the belt of his jeans as he threw his head back, watching her with the unblinking, cat-like stare which could be so disturbing. Emily felt a cold sweat break out along her back with the knowledge that she'd pushed Gavin far too firmly to the back of her mind, considering she'd been prepared to spend her life with the man only hours before. 'But then these things are all relative,' he purred in that raspy, velvety voice which made her fingers describe themselves into claws in her fists.

Hateful, hateful snake, she thought, squaring her shoulders. His self-appointed task was to torment! 'I want to go home.'

'What home?' he enquired brutally.

'Happy about that, are you? As a matter of fact I'm without a job, too. Gavin was being...is being transferred to Paris, so I refused the job they offered me as a probationary teacher. That should make you wildly ecstatic. It does occur to me that now I've been symbolically disowned there is little point in my staying here. I can't see there's much more damage you can do.' There was, but she wasn't about to tell him about that.

'Maybe I want you here,' he replied swiftly in a goaded tone that was difficult to decipher.

'And risk being contaminated by a Stapely?' she replied huskily. If he had wanted her... The unbidden thought brought a tide of desolation. 'I won't be some sacrificial lamb, Luke,' she warned him.

'What did you have in mind to place on the altar, Emmy? Your body? I refused the offer of that once before,' he reminded her crudely. 'I feel sure all this emotional excess has exhausted you.' He flung a sleeping-bag at her, which she automatically caught. 'I've only got around to making one bedroom habitable. Don't look so stricken, infant,' he sneered. 'There's a folding thing in the dressing-room, just about your size.'

The reminder of her youthful indiscretion made her wince. Subtlety had not been high on the agenda; her imagination had taken over completely that summer to the point where she had convinced herself that her feelings were fully reciprocated. He had to have noticed, of course, but this was the first time he'd referred to it. That in itself, now she came to think about it, was surprising. She lowered her eyes to conceal to what extent the memory could still mortify her.

'Where?' she asked stiffly.

'Top of the stairs, bathroom's to the left.' He watched her climb the stairs, her back stiff, the drift of honey hair across her face hiding her expression from his view. Once she was out of sight his shoulders sagged, the lines of exhaustion on his face deepening. He reached into a cupboard, pulled out a bottle of malt whisky and covered the bottom of a tumbler with the liquid. He drained it in one gulp, grimacing, and stood watching the staircase, his expression one of frustrated self-disgust.

CHAPTER FOUR

BY THE TIME Emily had made up the bed she could barely keep her eyes open. Not bothering to search her overnight bag for a nightdress, she slid out of her clothes and, wearing only a pair of brief pants, slipped inside the sleeping-bag. She embraced the dark oblivion of sleep as it washed insistently over her.

She dreamt, and it was disturbing enough for her to surface, her throat raw with screams that rent the silence with jagged, serrated tears. The content had vanished, leaving only profound fear. As a child, and then again in her teens, she had often woken this way; but not for a long time now. Her body shook spasmodically as if gripped by a fever.

She sat up, her skin slick and clammy, and, fumbling, she reached for an unfamiliar switch in the darkness. Her hand touched something warm, human, she gave a fresh shriek and the room was illuminated in subdued light that seemed intense to her night vision.

'Calm down.' Luke loomed over her, tall and dark, his face harsh and taut in the shadows.

He sounded angry, probably at having his sleep interrupted, she thought, reality seeping through the miasma of nebulous dread.

In a flash the essential details of her nightmare were upon her. Luke making love to the blonde, herself unable to move in the doorway, her juvenile fantasies disintegrating around her, the sound of their laughter like sandpaper on her nerve-endings. She'd felt deeply betrayed, humiliated.

The present had in some way thrown her into a time warp, at least while she slumbered and her subconscious came out to play. It would have been easy to dismiss the reminder of a youthful crush, but not so easy to dismiss the taste of pain and humiliation this ghost from the past could still summon after all these years. The passion, the obsessive craving, it had faded over the years, leaving behind an antagonism, a wariness of Luke she no longer traced to its source. Had she permitted herself to experience anything as strong since?

A scream was still caught in her throat like an aching solid thing. She fought for composure, her lungs making a laboured bid to draw oxygen. The bed creaked as Luke lowered himself on to the edge. Emily opened her eyes, which seemed too large in her drawn, finely boned face, the sweep of dark lashes throwing a shadow across her cheekbones.

'Sorry I woke you.' Her voice was husky; the effort of appearing normal was physically painful. She wanted Luke to go away and leave her to give in to the avalanche of misery that demanded release. She couldn't do so in front of him—through the pain that one fact remained uppermost. It was very important not to let Luke see her pain, use her weakness to form his weapons of ridicule and scorn.

His brows drew together in a fierce, violent frown. 'For God's sake, stop looking so damned noble and let go,' he snarled with brutal impatience. He grabbed her by the shoulders and pulled her towards him. She was too shocked to protest as she found herself drawn roughly against his chest. It wasn't tenderness, but it was enough to liberate her feelings. He allowed her sobs to run their course until only an occasional hiccup of misery shook her limp frame.

Feeling him shift made Emily aware that his tolerance was wearing thin. Almost at the same instant as she squirmed to push herself away she became aware of other previously overlooked details. She was the next best thing to naked and her breasts were in close contact with a hair-roughened chest. The sensation was a first; she couldn't believe it had taken her this long to appreciate the abrasive contact. She felt her flesh acknowledge flagrantly the intimacy of her situation.

With an inarticulate sound of dismay she pulled away. This broke the tactile embarrassment, but rather too late she realised that it revealed her to his unashamedly interested eyes. The blue gaze flickered from her flushed face down to the gentle sway of her breasts, pearly pale in the subdued light, gleaming with an opalescence that made Luke's breathing grow shallower. He seemed transfixed by the sight; his eyes followed the blue tracery of veins that were visible through the skin. The expression in his eyes was primitively ferocious

It was as if she was immobilised by the onslaught of his silent gaze. A robe, black, knotted loosely at the waist and gaping where her head had moments before lain, was all he appeared to be wearing. Involuntarily her eyes slid down the length of his legs, darkly tanned, covered with a dusting of dark hair. She made the return journey with an unfocused, dazed expression, trying to blot out the impact of the muscular power of his thighs on her senses.

She was trying to analyse the paroxysm of sensation that was aggravating every nerve-ending in her body. Luke's eyes, glowing with a frightening intensity, made her instantaneously aware of an important part of his personality—the earthy sensuality that suddenly hit her with a stunning force.

Her mind was a disorganised maze of impressions, half-formed concepts; she longed for solitude to allow these things to develop undisturbed by the analysis—the knowledge—she could see in the sapphire stare. Why did Luke always seem to know something she didn't?

'He's not worth dreaming about,' he said tightly.

'He?' She stared at him blankly. He was talking about

Gavin, she realised, interpreting his words incredulously. She ought to have been dreaming of her ex-fiancé.

She was still sitting there, her nakedness on display, and the realisation came with a surge of blood that stained her skin. Shaking, she clutched at the sleeping-bag, pulling it up to her chin. Her knees went up to her chest and she hugged her arms protectively around herself.

'It was just a nightmare,' she said huskily, feeling obliged to infuse a touch of normality into the proceedings—not that there was the first thing normal in Luke's sitting half naked on her bed!

The expression on his face as he watched her frenzied efforts at concealment made her feel even more flustered and unsophisticated. Women were seen topless around countless pools and on numerous beaches; she should have been able to deal with the situation with more panache, more finesse.

It wasn't being caught disrobed, it was being caught by Luke. She digested this insight with unease. If Gavin had discovered her in a similar situation she wouldn't have felt this acute painful awareness of her body; she'd have laughed the incident off and probably fought off his easily subdued advances. Luke wasn't about to make any advances to a Stapely, she reminded herself, unless, as earlier, he wanted to prove a point. A surge of adrenalin made her heart step up a beat as she skimmed over the idea. He wouldn't... She'd never... Was this really her feeling the heat of excitement as she speculated about the unthinkable? What would it feel like to have him touch her skin...?

'Was it a bad nightmare?'

Which one? she wondered with self-derisive irony. She tensed, startled by the fact that his soft words had set up a chain reaction that was trying to make her relax and accept the languor, incited by his casual enquiry. It had nothing to do with the content of his words; it was just a gut response to the sound of his voice. Luke didn't actually care, she reminded herself; he was a man devoid of humanity and compassion. He was using her, which was fine, because she would only use him. What was not fine was this inexplicable arrival in her erotically arid life of a tenacious thread of interest. She mentally corrected herself—interest was too insipid a term to describe the reluctant fascination that was in danger of turning the silken thread to steel bonds which would cut deep into her native inhibitions and sense of self-preservation. At all costs she wanted to avoid any repeat obsessiveness.

'I don't know.' Her voice sounded staccato and disconnected, as though the words held no meaning. 'I mean, I never remember; it's just the impression I'm left with. I'm fine now.' She gave a nervous laugh which hit the high ceiling and disintegrated into a series of small half-echoes.

'You look a little feverish.'

Her eyes, which had been skittering around the small room, avoiding his face, returned. He returned her suspicious glare with calm impassivity and she began to feel paranoid, reading innuendo in the simple statement. Did he know about the overheated core of irrational attraction she was futilely trying to subdue, trying to rationalise?

'It's a warm night,' she responded gruffly, striving to sound prosaic and unaffected by the impact his physical presence was having on her body and mind. He continued to watch her silently, his brilliant eyes smiling in a way she found profoundly troubling. It was as if he knew exactly what thoughts were passing through her mind.

He stretched with casual elegance, the smooth motion making the robe gape even more, revealing a flat, muscled belly. Emily was mortified to find her eyes riveted on his body; her breath came in shallow gasps as she fought to combat a hectic, light-headed, drugged sensation that swept over her in waves.

What is happening to me? she wondered. She closed her eyes and tried to bring the turbulent, uncontrolled sensations under control. 'You must be tired. I'm sorry I disturbed you, but I'm fine now.' She was pleased at her pleasant, level tone, more polite than she habitually used with Luke but better than the semi-hysterical plea that had trembled on her tongue. Why didn't he just go away, leave her in peace? she thought resentfully.

'It would be no trouble to stay,' he responded after a short pause.

Startled, her eyes shot to his face. He had imbued the offer with a wealth of meaning which was startlingly obvious. The cerulean gaze was brimming with mocking laughter and a speculative warmth that she chose to ignore, clinging instead to the mortification that stiffened her spine and made her quiver.

He knew exactly what effect his presence was having on her, and it was probably providing him with a wealth of malignant amusement. To imagine that he wasn't accustomed to exploiting his spell-binding looks to his own advantage, for his own amusement, would have been unrealistic. She gave herself a fierce mental shake to stop the warm, sluggish feelings, and wrapped justified anger around her.

'I don't think even you would take a joke that far,' she sneered. 'Besides, I respect you far too much to allow you to be a substitute,' she insinuated silkily. She met his glittering stare, her chin at a defiant angle. For a brief, painful second she indulgently allowed herself to recall the kiss earlier. It was something she had deliberately sealed away, refusing to acknowledge, and the lingering sense of intimacy, of things awoken and unfinished savagely kicked into life, made her sure she had to forget the incident.

'Death before dishonour?' he suggested softly, laughing as she flinched away from the casual touch of his thumb against her throat. 'Or shall we say frustration?' he suggested silkily.

'I'm far too tired for riddles,' she spat back. Inwardly his effortless perception appalled her.

'I was merely offering the comfort of my presence should your night terrors return.'

'I'd need to be seriously disturbed to accept comfort from someone incapable of distinguishing between affection and lust!' she retorted, her anger equally dividing between herself for being receptive at the worst moment possible to Luke's challenging sexuality, and him for enjoying it and not even having the common decency to disguise the fact.

'At least I've never been prepared to accept the former as a basis for marriage,' he responded with an edge of impatient contempt.

She went white and her fingers lost their grip on the sleeping-bag. 'How dare you?' she breathed wrathfully.

'Easily,' he replied casually. He reached out and hitched up the sleeping-bag to cover her half-exposed breasts. 'You really shouldn't flaunt the goods if they're not on the market,' he admonished crudely, with a scorn that made her flinch even more than the brief instant of contact as his knuckles had brushed her skin.

'Now that I'm here—a purely temporary situation—I'd like to emphasise that this...arrangement is one of convenience only.'

His eyebrows shot up and he gave a mirthless grin. 'How much more convenient could you require?'

'If you think I could find it anything other than repugnant to sleep with you, you're even more egotistically deluded than I had imagined!' she snapped back. She couldn't be sure whether he was pursuing this absurd avenue just to enjoy watching her squirm, or whether...and the idea made the pit of her belly disintegrate, leaving a warm, empty nothingness which ached dully. He wasn't actually serious...he couldn't be. Perhaps, she thought, her mind spinning, he was the sort of man who felt obliged to explore every avenue of conquest almost out of habit.

'Is that a fact?' he taunted, his eyes sardonic on her flushed face.

Emily felt as if guilt was written all over her face. She'd been engaged for over eight months to Gavin and never in all that time had she had any trouble resisting his attempts to become her lover. He'd seemed inclined to make a big thing of her desire to wait, not anticipate their marriage vows. If she could show restraint, she hadn't understood why he couldn't follow suit. She'd imagined their relationship had been based on more than a fleeting physical attraction, but then she'd thought a lot of things that had proved to be untrue.

Now here she was experiencing some sort of hormonal redress for her years of abstinence, and the catalyst was Luke, of all people. She could imagine the cynical amusement if he ever realised just how impoverished sexually her life had been. The feeling of horror eclipsed all other sensations as she dwelt on this prospect. No, she would preserve what little dignity she had—at least in front of her provoking saviour. After all, how hard could it be to subdue a bit of juvenile, sweaty-skinned pulse-racing? She had once before. She wasn't the sort of person who was a victim of her appetites. More importantly, she was no longer a wide-eyed teenager; she was a mature, sensible woman.

Her satisfaction at this hasty conclusion was somewhat ambiguous. Her body felt too alive, too inflamed for her not to experience a certain perverse frustration which she steadfastly refused to acknowledge.

'I realise I'm a convenient body, Luke,' she said drily, only too well aware that this was the only reason he had even noticed she was female. 'But it would take more than propinquity to induce me to seek dubious solace in your arms.' She kept a firm grip on the sleeping-bag to prevent it obeying gravity.

He listened to her with apparent interest. 'Propinquity wasn't doing badly a few moments ago, infant. I mean, I don't precisely object to being ogled like a sex object...' He watched the hot colour wash over her skin, his lips twisted into a sneer.

Emily was trying desperately to reconcile the truth in his cruel statement with the denial she longed to throw at him. 'You have a lurid imagination,' she said stiltedly. She knew all about imagination. There had been a time when it had been more real to her than reality.

He got up with a fluid movement that made her tense; it was impossible not to be aware of the innate grace that was impressive in such a large man. He exhibited such a harmony of controlled strength that it was difficult, in her state of heightened awareness, not to watch him covertly, almost angrily, from beneath her eyelashes.

'I expect Gavin is finding comfort at this moment in the arms of the delectable Charlotte,' he taunted, his voice apparently savouring the picture this observation conjured up, a picture which made Emily face once more the disaster of her failure...failure to hold the interest of the man she had been set to spend her entire life with. 'If your taste runs to Barbie dolls, she must seem heaven-sent. I was just offering you the opportunity to enjoy the same solace.'

'That's incredibly chivalrous of you, Luke, but I couldn't impose on your good nature,' she replied with savage irony.

He met her angry glare with infuriating blandness as he casually turned the door-handle. 'One thing, Emily. I suggest you put something on—just in case you should happen to succumb to another nightmare.' His eyes slid away from her face and she became aware of a sudden tension in him, in the harsh lines of his face, a raw flicker of blue fire that smouldered into life in his eyes. 'I wouldn't put too much faith in my good nature, if I were you.'

Shivering, Emily sat on the bed, assailed by a torrent of doubts. There had been a definite warning in that parting shot, a hint of the ruthlessness she knew Luke to possess. She was suddenly directly in the firing line in this war of attrition. In this small engagement she had almost become a symbol of overall victory. She was just beginning to appreciate the dangers inherent in such a position.

She might have outgrown childish infatuations, but she knew better than to underestimate youthful passion. To face up to the absurdity of her lurid imaginings had been the most painful experience of her life. What am I thinking? she reprimanded herself. Today is the worst day of my life—how can I possibly compare a humiliation four years old to the wholesale betrayal by the people closest to me?

It was sensible to put down her erratic and explosive awareness of Luke to her shattering discoveries, discoveries which had thrown her life off course. She rejected firmly any other possible explanation.

Comforting herself with this conclusion, she tried to drift back to sleep, her head buried in the sleeping-bag—but not before she'd extracted a nightshirt from her hastily packed case. Her thoughts touched on the moment she'd become aware of the skin-to-skin contact. Her mind soon blanked out the episode, but she had already recalled the texture...the imprint of a hard male body.

If Luke had been serious when he'd suggested they spend the night together, and she had been crazy enough to give in to some aberrant weakness, she doubted whether she'd have spared much time worrying over Gavin, she admitted to herself, unable to deny the fact that there was something about Luke that could make other aspects of life, even crucial ones, fade into insignificance. In the darkness her eyes shot open. She hadn't, though, had she? Her muddled thoughts had been revolving around her disagreeable distant relation, not her former fiancé.

She closed her eyes and determinedly constructed a sensation of self-pity and betrayal, finding this pit of misery less menacing than her previous mental meanderings.

'TEA, AND TOAST.'

Emily blinked. The brief knock on the adjoining door had given her little time to gather her sleepy wits. Luke bore down upon her, balancing a tray on one hand. His comprehensive glance made her conscious of her tousled hair and no doubt ravaged face. She hitched the loose night-shirt up over the shoulder it had slipped down and sat up self-consciously.

The tray was placed across her knees. 'I've not laced anything with hallucinagenic drugs,' he assured her drily as she stared suspiciously at the food. He lifted the lid on a pot. 'Preserve, not arsenic.'

He picked up the bundle of clothes she'd laid across the one chair in the small room and put them on the floor. He proceeded to pick up the chair and straddle it, his hands on the wooden slatted back. He regarded her silent figure quiz-zically.

'Thank you,' she managed. His manner was amazingly commonplace considering the exchanges which had taken place in the early hours.

'It was considerate of me, wasn't it?' he agreed with a complacent grin.

Her frown deepened. 'I can do without an audience.' It was considerate if you didn't take into account the fact that he'd tricked her into being here, miles away from civilisa-tion. The less her mind dwelt on his behaviour since they had arrived, the better for her composure; and as for the revelations about her own father's part in his mother's death... She sighed and sipped the tea. Any overtures of friendship had to be treated for what they would always be—a covert means to perpetuate the vendetta.

'Are you always so ratty in the morning?' he enquired with a humorous quirk to his lips. 'Or does it all depend on the night before...? I can recommend a run for frustra-tion. It does wonders.'

The casual reference, the implication that he was frustrated, made her relinquish the slender hold she had over her composure. She noticed the damp stain in the centre of his T-shirt where the material displayed the sculpted outline of his musculature, and she swallowed a stricture in her throat.

'If it weren't for you I'd be in a comfortable hotel bed, not on this thing,' she said disparagingly. Attack seemed the easiest option at this point. 'I hold you directly responsible for my lack of sleep.'

An expression flickered at the back of his eyes. 'And I hold you directly responsible for mine,' he said simply. He flexed his shoulders and rubbed his neck. 'My bed is far more commodious... Keep it in mind.'

He was totally outrageous, she decided, extricating her eyes from the subtly altered expression in his blue orbs. She tried to speak but all that emerged was a hoarse squeak.

'Aren't you going to eat? After all the trouble I went to.'

'I seem to recall something about Greeks bearing gifts.' The complacent grin at her inarticulate display made her bristle defensively. 'Where did the food come from, anyway?'

'A friend very kindly stocks up for me when I let her know I'm coming.'

'Very neighbourly,' she observed sourly. The gender of the neighbour came as no shock to her. 'The note on the table...'

'Was from Beth. A very good-natured girl, Beth,' he mused, his eyes on her face.

Did Beth rate breakfast in bed? she wondered cynically, relatively certain that she didn't like this treasure.

'You could have met if she hadn't had to go to London. As you're so interested.'

'Devastating news,' she muttered drily.

'I expect you're delighted at having me to yourself.'

She dropped the spoon of blackcurrant preserve and glared at him. 'I don't want you. In fact, I don't even want to share you,' she corrected him. 'All I want is to get out of here,' she informed him, giving a growl of fury as the only response to her insistence was one of amusement. 'You don't seem to take any of this seriously.'

'On the contrary, Emmy, I take this very seriously. You, on the other hand, don't appear to appreciate the unique honour of being here. I never bring women here,' he told her blandly.

'Of which there are many, no doubt,' she said bitterly.

'Do I detect a certain green tinge, infant?' he drawled.

She felt the cursed colour stain her cheeks and took a deep, steadying breath. 'Sympathy is all you're likely to detect. The last four years, which, in case you've forgotten, have been Luke-free for me, have been blissful.' She conveniently forgot the time during that first year when she'd scoured the news items that evenly remotely concerned him. Not to mention being glued to the TV screen when he presented the award-winning report on the Kurdish refugees.

'Yes, I noticed how ecstatically happy you were when the mascara was running in rivulets down your cheeks. Shame I had to breeze in and spoil all that undiluted hilarity.'

She averted her face, sharply inhaling and controlling an urge to lash out blindly. 'That was just in case I'd forgotten what a mess my life was in.'

'Emily, tell me, have you thought of Gavin once today?'

Shock rippled deep inside her and gradually slid into her wide eyes. 'Of course I have.' He knew she was lying and so did she, but the pretence seemed important. She had to perpetuate it, delay the moment when she'd have to face up to things she was avoiding. 'Anyway, I doubt if the sort of women you go around with would care for a place with no possibility of a photo opportunity,' she said sarcastically, taking a sharp U-turn. 'Being seen with you is probably just a smart career move for them. I had no idea you were such a compulsive property buyer anyway. What do you need with—what is it?—four homes anyway?'

'Could be I hate hotels; or maybe it's a reaction to the days I didn't have a roof.'

This statement made her frown in confusion, her guard dropping for a moment. 'I don't understand, Luke… How…when were you homeless?'

Luke's face was very still, carved, beautiful but without life, almost like a statue, but his eyes were intensely alive, as if he could recall with clarity the days she was puzzling over. 'I was put in a home when she died,' he told her abruptly. His eyes flicked to her face, holding her gaze. The slow warmth of compassion that softened her wide eyes brought an angry sneer to his lips.

She lowered her eyelashes, strangely hurt by the rejection of her instinctive sympathy. She blinked back the burn of unshed tears and wondered whether they had been incited by pity or a genuine, unexpected concern she was experiencing for this abrasive, independent man. If the latter was true, she thought with confusion, she would do well to stifle such notions at birth because even the idea of Luke's rebuffs at her anxiety for his welfare made her recoil.

'I left before they traced your parents. I'd been on the street for a year before I was sucked back into the system and the loving bosom of your family.'

She digested this information and the bleakness behind the economic description. She was deeply horrified by the details she knew must lurk behind the succinct history. The air of barely suppressed truculence she could vaguely remember about him seemed easier to understand; the defiance and sometimes calculated indifference which had managed to alienate the adults in her family—had that been a result of the early traumas, and not just his insurgent personality?

To the secure, middle-class world she had known he had been a threat, not accepting the concepts of authority which it had never occurred to her to question. She wondered how school had reacted to the blue-eyed belligerence he had carried with him. If her experience was anything to go by it wouldn't have been favourable, but at least he had had an intellect which would, at least in academic circles, have excused his nonconformist attitudes.

'Why did you run away?'

'Could be I react badly to authority.' He shrugged. 'I didn't care to be analysed by a bunch of establishment do-gooders.'

'They are there to help. A safety-net for kids like you.'

'I wasn't *like* anything; I was myself, Emily. I preferred, and still do, to sort my problems out in my own way. I can't say I can look back upon that period of my life with affection, but it taught me some important lessons. I learnt to be self-reliant.'

'You don't need anyone, then?' she taunted. 'You never let anyone near you.' There was no compromise in Luke. She'd always known that he lived life on his own terms and would never consider making concessions. It made her inordinately angry just to think it.

'You mean when I was welcomed into the warm, loving bosom of your family?' He made a derisive sound in his throat. 'How hard do you think they looked for me, Emily?' he asked harshly, and she couldn't hold his ironic gaze. 'Possibly they might have forgiven me for being who I was if I had been sufficiently grateful for all the crumbs they flung in my direction,' he drawled. 'To their credit, it was all so subtly done—the message that Luke would never amount to anything. The subliminal message was in every glance, every word. They had to provide for me, of course, if only because it fitted in with the big-hearted, altruistic image your father has fashioned for himself. A bit like the amounts of money he donates to charities, which just happen to find their way into the Press,' he said scornfully.

It had never occurred to her to consider Luke a victim

before; he was the one who could do everything, always succeeded. She had envied his freedom from the need to conform. He was ultimately himself, never seeking approval from a soul. He must have resented his second-class status, an almost segregated position in the hierarchy of the household. She'd seen him as her brother's rival, the thorn in her parents' side, and had never, she realised, looked at things from his side of the fence.

'I'm sorry.' She winced: it was woefully inadequate.

'What for, Emmy? Having a pony, being chauffeur-driven to school and having anything you mentioned wistfully magically materialise?'

'The spoilt brat syndrome, I know,' she snapped back angrily. 'What Daddy loves, you loathe. That's it, isn't it? Do I have to suffer some sort of degradation before I am considered for the Lucas Hunt register of acceptable persons? I'd have thought being here with you would be readily classified as suffering and degradation of a severe variety,' she sneered. 'But then, it's supposed to, isn't it, Luke?' The impetuous, agitated movement sent the tray crashing to the floor, and unexpectedly and without warning she began to cry, tears seeping silently from her eyes and sliding down her cheeks.

Luke stared at her, his blue eyes ablaze. He shook his head in a negative gesture of denial. 'You've not the faintest idea what you're talking about,' he said huskily.

She glared back through the glitter of tears, ignoring the air of suspended violence in him, the clenched jaw and rampant glow in his eyes that should have made her subside. 'I'm not that stupid, Luke. My dilemma fell into your lap like a gift from the gods, didn't it?' she accused. 'The only mistake I made was not realising how irrelevant I, as a person, am to you... how far you'd actually go to wreak some sort of vengeance. You'd actually make love to me, wouldn't you, to hit back? Although love would be the wrong word, wouldn't it?' For a moment her voice was completely suspended by tears. She ignored the low growl that was emitted from his throat, a raw, primal sound that made the hairs on the nape of her neck stand on end.

'What had you intended doing, Luke? Closing your eyes and composing your poisonous taunts? No greater sacrifice has man…I'm sure your mother would have been proud. Your touch makes my skin crawl,' she added with defiance. 'I suggest you think of some other method to achieve the ultimate revenge, because I sure as hell am not going to co-operate!'

His feet crunched the broken china into powder as he strode towards her. His hands closed around her skull as he sat on the edge of the narrow bed. His face was terrifyingly furious as he focused on her, and the power in his hands as his fingers tightened forced her up to her knees.

'Go on,' she taunted. 'Hate me by association. At least that's honest, instead of pretending…'

'Pretending what?' His voice was husky, almost unsteady as his eyes flared at her studied, desperate insolence.

'Pretending you find me attractive,' she spat out. 'I'm not that stupid, you know. It's about the ultimate humiliation to be a pawn. It makes me feel soiled.'

The blue eyes were reaching melting-point and instinctively she tried to draw back, but his fingers had wrapped themselves into the strands of her hair and the effort made her whimper in pain.

'You're a liar,' he snarled as his pupils dilated, almost obliterating the cerulean colour of the twin points of fire. 'That's not the way my touch makes you feel…' His words thudded into her with the same intensity as the drowning sound of her heartbeat pounding in her ears. She closed her eyes on a soundless cry of protest as his mouth sought her trembling lips. The harsh sound of his breathing was loud in her ears, and she heard the swift, ragged moan of his painfully ragged inhalation as she opened her mouth for his invasive tongue. The sound and the touch made her knees crumble. He fell with her to the bed and they lay thigh to thigh, breast to breast…heart to heart.

The hunger, the driving, empty hunger was all-consuming; it had found a corresponding need in the aggressive masculinity of him that was pushing her to fever pitch. Hands in his hair, lips on his skin, she was muttering a series of inarticulate pleas, unaware that her mouth issued the soft noises. The forays of his tongue in her moist mouth were alternately teasing and plundering, while his hands moving over her body made her aware of a vital sensuality, a pleasure in the intense sensations he was evoking with the slightest butterfly touch on a vulnerable area.

'Soiled, Emily?' His voice, husky, slurred, was almost unrecognisable. For a moment he examined her flushed, shocked face, his eyes incandescent. A groan was wrenched from his throat as he felt her flinch. He rolled over on to his side and, running unsteady hands through his tousled dark hair, levered himself from the low divan. 'If you're going to attack me with the unvarnished truth, infant, make sure it's just that,' he said, showing no mercy for her sharp gasp of anguish. 'If it's any comfort, I don't choose to—' she saw his throat work as his eyes ran with a compulsive need he was obviously fighting over her body, clothed only in the brief nightshirt '—respond to you,' he finished throatily. He bent forward and lifted a hank of her thick hair, letting it slide silkily through his fingers, his expression almost abstracted as he did so.

Emily felt pleasure; nerve-endings craving contact purred into warm life at his touch. The impulse had no consciousness behind it; it was a response to the erotic glow still engulfing her, sheer spontaneity. She took his wrist in both her hands and, turning his fist palm upwards, pressed her lips to the skin.

His head jerked back as though she'd struck him and his breath whistled out with a sibilant hiss. 'What is this, infant, role reversal?'

Her hands had already fallen away. Miserably aware of how wide she'd opened herself for his retributive attack, she lowered her eyes. 'I wanted…' She bit her lip. How to make things worse, she thought; I could write the definitive book.

'In an hour's time, maybe two, you'd accuse me of sleeping with you to satisfy my unhealthy desire for revenge.'

She looked up, startled into animation, her sense of self-preservation reawakened by her persecutor, of all people. 'You can't deny it would be awfully convenient.' Had that been his intention all along when he'd tricked her into coming her? 'How far in advance do you plan your strategy, Luke?'

'You are so bloody predictable,' he flung at her, his expression cynically furious. 'I can almost see the wheels turning.'

'Predictable!' she fumed, looping the nightshirt once more over her shoulder, aware that his eyes were repeatedly drawn to the curve of her shoulder. 'It's you who are predictable,' she cried, torn between wanting to respond to the primitive gleam of hunger in his eyes and an instinct not to take anything he said or did at face value. 'You'll do whatever it takes to hurt my father.' The anger died away and a deep sadness replaced it in her upturned face. 'I don't think you take prisoners, do you, Luke? Not in the rules of combat.' She gave a small shrug. I'm irrelevant, she kept telling herself, a tool, a weapon. Don't be a victim of your own wishful thinking, Emily—hate him. She needed to hate Luke.

'If that were true, Emily, I'd have taken you when you were sixteen. You looked at me as though you'd die just to have me touch you,' he recalled, a nerve throbbing in his lean cheek with erratic force. 'Think about that and try to recall you have the most expressive eyes I've ever seen in my life.' He spoke in slow, measured tones, and then he was gone.

CHAPTER FIVE

'MAKING YOURSELF useful?'

Emily didn't flinch but continued to type, slowly transcribing the tightly packed writing in the notebook. She'd heard Luke's footsteps as he'd entered the room. She could smell the scent of fresh air, peat and the sea that hung about him.

'I don't want to be accused of sponging off your hospitality, do I?' she drawled sarcastically without looking up. Actually, it helped to have something else to concentrate on, something to divert her thoughts. 'Or don't you like anyone to see the embryo?'

'I've no objection to that, just your tone.'

'We aim to give offence,' she said cheerfully.

He slammed his hand down over her fingers on the keyboard. 'I wouldn't advise it.'

She lifted her face then and stared at him with unflinching scorn. 'I didn't ask to come here. If you don't like my company, take me to the nearest sign of civilisation. I've walked a mile in every direction and a sheep is the only sign of life I came across.'

'Such initiative, infant,' he said silkily. 'If you'd bothered to ask, I could have told you Beth is our nearest neighbour and she lives in the friendly neighbourhood castle…five miles as the crow flies and seven by road.'

'You weren't here to ask,' she replied, depressed by this information. She had dressed slowly, putting off the inevitable return match once she came downstairs. It had been an anticlimax when she had discovered she was quite alone in the cottage.

'You missed me. I'm touched.'

She got up and turned to face him. Even at full stretch she barely topped his shoulder. 'You can't keep me prisoner, Luke,' she challenged him.

'What you can't do is wander off around here, Emmy. It's not Hyde Park. It's very easy to get lost if you don't know what you're doing.'

She made a sound of frustration. 'Your concern is very touching, but you still haven't answered my question.'

His blue eyes regarded her steadily. 'What question? You made a statement, typically incorrect. You're my guest, not a prisoner, and you're here until I choose to take you elsewhere.'

Her eyes sizzled. 'That's an outrageous thing to say. You won't *take* me anywhere? You make me sound like a bag of flour! As for guest, prisoner, it's all semantics. I'm here against my will; in my book that means you abducted me.'

'My dearest Emily,' he said as though her outrage were completely unexpected, 'if you're that bothered, telephone home, call out the rescue parties.'

She stared at him. 'Telephone…?'

'You want a dictionary definition or a technical explanation?'

'You actually have a telephone here?' she said incredulously. Why hadn't that occurred to her?

'In case of emergencies.'

'Where?'

'In the bedroom; didn't you notice?' he mocked.

She flushed. She had walked through his room with her eyes downcast; the presence of the kingsize bed and the personal clutter had been too painfully evocative of the room's owner for her to linger. 'I want to telephone Dad; he'll be worried.'

'Feel free.'

She frowned. His reaction was too co-operative to make sense. 'What are you up to?'

'I'm trying to lure you into my bedroom and make passionate love to you.'

'Don't be stupid.' The sensation that sizzled along her nerve-endings was appallingly strong. She made an effort to subdue the erotic images that his words had sparked off in her head.

'True,' he agreed thoughtfully. Then, meeting the chagrin she couldn't keep from showing in her eyes, he grinned. 'I don't think we'd make it up the stairs, Emmy.' The tone was clinical, the insolent smoulder in his eyes anything but.

Emily gulped, hating the sensation that was liquid heat seeping through her. She was as helpless as a moth drawn to the warmth and inevitable doom of a glowing flame. 'You do think a lot of yourself, don't you?'

'A less resilient soul would have had his confidence pounded into dust at the tender mercies of the Stapely clan,' he confirmed.

'You never *tried* to fit in,' she accused.

'I only make concessions for people who would do the same for me.'

The most constant of friends, but cross him and beware! This wasn't news to her. 'Why are you encouraging me to ring Dad, Luke?' She watched the cold smile curve his lips and wondered how she had been so dense. 'You want me to do your dirty work for you. If I ring Dad, saying you kidnapped me…'

'The response would be gratifyingly extreme, I'd say.'

Emily stopped dead. 'You are so vindictive, so callous…you disgust me!' She mounted the stairs, wishing she could feel resigned to his coercion. But it hurt…it hurt badly.

The telephone was on the slate-topped wash-stand. She pushed aside the assorted pile of books that almost obscured it from view. Dialling her father's number, she tried to compose herself. She owed it to him at least to let him know she was alive. She'd been angry with him, and, though in the heat of that anger she might have wished him suffering, she never had been able to sustain any vindictive sentiments. She'd do that but not Luke's dirty work. The fact that he could manoeuvre her so cold-bloodedly incensed her, made her want to scream at him.

'Emily, is that you?' She heard the deep sigh of relief echo down the line. 'Where the hell are you? Are you with him…?'

She didn't need to ask who he meant. 'I'm fine, Dad…I just need time to think.'

'Alone?'

'I have seen Luke,' she said carefully. The language that greeted this statement was colourful. With resignation Emily let the stream of abuse run its course.

'Come home, Emily… You don't have to marry Gavin, you don't have to marry anyone. But come home.'

Emily swallowed. It was as close as she'd ever heard her father come to pleading. 'That's not possible right now.' She'd expected to be chastised as if she were some wayward adolescent—that was the usual. She realised he must be really worried. She shook her head, trying to clear emotional fog that made it difficult to think clearly.

She raised her hand with the receiver in it and brushed it across her clammy forehead. A cry of surprise slipped from her lips as the instrument was extracted from her light clasp. She leapt to her feet, but Luke held it out of her reach and fended her off easily with one hand.

After a brief struggle she found he had somehow clamped her to his side, her hands caught between her own body and his. She continued to struggle wildly even though she knew the effort was futile; it was like being held by steel bands.

'You drew blood, you little cat,' he observed, his eyes flashing when she eventually subsided.

'Good,' she spat, seeing the discoloured marks on his hand. 'Give it back!'

Luke's eyes were focused on her lips, which were full, trembling with emotion. With an apparent effort he angrily tore them away. 'All in good time,' he said, his face dangerously lacking expression, completely under iron control once more. 'Charlie, are you still there?' he said, lifting his hand from the receiver. He held it a few inches away from his ear, his eyebrows shooting heavenwards. 'He is,' he confirmed to Emily, who kicked his shin. He grimaced and spoke into the phone once more. 'Static on the line; sorry about that. You really mustn't worry about Emily. I'll take very good care of her. I can see you've got the wrong impression, Charlie,' he said after a short pause. 'My intentions are entirely honourable, if that's what's worrying you. To be honest, I've been thinking for some time I should be settling down.'

Emily gave a whimper of pure disbelief and her body sagged against him. It was just as well that the story of her father's heart condition had been greatly exaggerated, she thought with bitter irony.

Luke gave a puzzled sigh. 'The great man hung up,' he announced, returning the receiver to its cradle. 'Was it something I said?'

Emily slid from his loosened grip. 'Well, I hope you're finally satisfied,' she said, feet apart, her hands resting on the curve of her slender hips. 'The great manipulator at work. I'm impressed.'

'It was nothing really,' he said sardonically.

'I suppose you had it all planned down to the last disgusting syllable.'

'Only the vague outline. I was winging it,' he replied with a complacent smile that sent the blood rushing to her head. 'I must admit I'm modestly pleased with the outcome. I love to hear Charlie gibber; it has a bizarre charm.'

Hot colour suffused her cheeks and rage exploded in the confines of her head. 'You are the most disgusting, loathsome, despicable, twisted piece of slime!'

'I hate to interrupt you in full flow, but I'm curious to know just what precisely you object to. Gibber must run in the family,' he added half to himself.

She gasped. 'You can ask that? You manoeuvred me into making that phone call seem legitimate.'

'Considering you've been raised at Charlcot, I'm amazed how naïve you can be sometimes, Emmy. I simply told the truth.'

'Truth,' she muttered disparagingly. 'You wouldn't know it if you fell over it. That was a complete fabrication from beginning to end.'

'I recall distinctly that you said you'd prefer to marry me than Gavin.'

She snorted with derision. 'That's so typical of you. Take everything out of context, distort it.'

'It set me thinking,' he continued as though she hadn't spoken. 'What a good idea it would be, marriage to a Stapely, a member of the inner circle.' His sensual mouth curved cynically as he slipped off the bland mask; his eyes were searingly blue and as steely as his taut expression. 'It seems an ideal solution all round.'

She shuddered and stared at him with growing incredulity. Serious...it wasn't possible...not even Luke was that fixated, or unrealistic. 'Not from where I'm standing.' She gave a faint laugh. 'I feel stupid just acting as if you're serious, Luke; naïve I might be, but I've not got a drop of martyr's blood in my veins. I'd never, in any circumstances, marry you.'

'You were going to marry Gavin.'

'I love—' she began, only to be interrupted furiously.

'Fiction and you know it,' he bit back, his eyes examining her face with clinical detachment.

She couldn't bring herself to deny this; she never had loved Gavin, but that didn't make her willing to contemplate such an impossibly ridiculous proposition. 'You might have succeeded in bringing me here, Luke, but marrying me against my will might prove taxing even for your ingenuity. The whole thing is preposterous.' She couldn't quite believe he meant any of it. Any second now he would crack a joke—this was all part of his warped sense of humour.

'I don't find you boring, Emmy,' he said slowly, reflectively, his tone low, intimate, with husky, swirling depths that were incredibly seductive. A corner of his mouth lifted as she wrapped her arms around her body. 'And sexually speaking I find you one of the most sensual creatures alive. While it lasted, infant, we could have pleasure.'

She gave a startled gasp. His voice…just his voice had almost been enough to bewitch her, and then the pragmatic 'while it lasted' had awoken her to the criminal folly of listening to the sensual cravings of her wilful body.

'This is to be temporary, then, this marriage,' she said, carefully neutral.

'Most are, it seems to me,' he said harshly, frowning slightly at her sudden self-possession.

'And I take it liaisons—discreet, of course—would be acceptable.' She felt a small surge of confidence at his blank look. 'You see, although Gavin and I may not be meant to be lifetime partners, he was a very…satisfactory lover,' she announced gravely. 'I'm sure we could come to some civilised arrangement.'

She heard the sound of his teeth grate against one another and saw the gleaming, predatory expression steal across his face. 'My wife won't require another lover.'

He was awesome, she had to admit it. Something in her thrilled to the hawkish, wholly aggressive expression that had effectively blotted out the urbane, self-possessed man she knew. 'And I could never be satisfied by one man.' She was playing with fire, but it would be worth it. How dared he assume she was his for the taking, that she would be stupid enough to fall in with whatever scheme he proposed?

She was sure he was going to explode as he assimilated her provocative statement in stony silence. The austere disapproval transformed in the blink of an eye to laughter, sudden genuine laughter, deep and attractive. 'You're right, Emily, that wasn't a very attractive proposal. You were piqued…'

Piqued she was, appalled, insulted, though perhaps it had been ambitious to play games with the master of the art. 'You really are serious, aren't you?' Finally she was convinced. 'You'd actually marry because it's the most sophisticated form of torture you can conceive.'

His eyes narrowed at the look of disgust that contorted her features. 'What other reason could there be?'

His tone eluded her; he was evincing strong emotions she couldn't quite track to their source. 'I take it that was a rhetorical question,' she said bitterly. His words had the ability to stab.

He smiled and she immediately knew she was going to hate what he said. 'I wonder what Daddy would say if he knew his concern over his precious little girl was four years late? What, Emily, would Daddy think if he knew his little girl had slid into my bed all those years ago…right under his roof?' He watched the colour seep from her face and his expression didn't alter. 'I think on balance it would rate even higher in the humiliation stakes than marrying me now. What do you think?' he enquired.

Her eyes were wide, almost black with horror. This was indeed refined cruelty. 'We didn't…I didn't,' she said, shaking her head in denial. 'Luke…' The plea and confusion in her voice made his jaw tighten.

'I know that, infant, and so do you. But what we both

also know is that you thought about it.' He paused, allowing this to sink in fully. 'It's a little like the old problem: is adultery any less adultery when it remains in the imagination of two people?'

'Two...?' she echoed in a numb voice.

'You can't imagine I didn't know what you were thinking, offering, Emily,' he said harshly. 'A strange intimacy builds up gradually amid all that unspoken conspiracy of desire; even without words your intentions were incredibly articulate. It may surprise you to know I imagined it some too.'

This was so impossibly awful! She hadn't known mortification actually had a physical taste. He hadn't been able to stomach the thought at the time of sleeping with a Stapely, that much was obvious. Given his relentless pursuit of vengeance it was the only explanation of the fact that he'd never encouraged her to fulfil her cravings.

She gave a sudden groan and clutched her stomach, the knowledge that flashed through her brain actually manifesting itself in physical pain. She'd never escaped her juvenile fixation; it had matured with her. She was still in love with Luke—all the denial was never going to change that fact. He loathed her...enough to marry her. The bizarre irony of this fact made her laugh, straightening up as she did so.

'You really would sink that low?' Beads of sweat stood out on the marble paleness of her wide brow, and a nerve leapt in his cheek as his eyes ran assessingly over her.

'You have to think like scum to catch scum,' he said brutally. 'I think you'd better think over my proposal, Emily. The idea does have its merits...if you're honest.'

Honest! He could say the word without flinching. 'You're blackmailing me, Luke.'

'When I want something I'm prepared to go as far as required,' he said tautly.

'You really hate me that much? Or am I just insignificant, merely in the way?'

The curve of his mouth promised sensual delights, but his eyes were bitterly ironic, tired, weary eyes. 'Infant,' he said softly, his hand running through his hair not totally steady, 'I think you're essential to my plans.' He smiled, a mocking smile that seemed to be aimed at himself rather than her.

'You mean you need my collusion to deliver the ultimate punishment,' she accused, sure now that she was permanently off balance. She would never take anything at face value again!

'I think you should consider my proposal.'

'Ultimatum.'

Luke looked at her from beneath hooded eyelids. He made a circular motion with his head, rubbing his neck as if to relieve unseen knots in the columns of muscle and sinew. 'I won't argue with that,' he said shortly. He extended the motion, outlining the concave shape of his belly below the ridge of his ribs. She saw the bank of flesh across his waist and the beginning of the scar that ran across his back to terminate just to the right of his spine.

Completely distracted, she licked her dry lips, recalling the occasion she'd asked him about his wound, the one that had kept him so close during that fateful summer. He'd shown her then the line of puckered flesh, purple still from recent surgery to remove the shrapnel that had strayed perilously close to his spine.

He'd taken her reaction to be one of horror, whereas in reality the physical evidence of his pain had not repelled her at all. It was the reminder of how close to death or permanent disability he had come that had made her grow cold with fear. The fact that he'd had pain had made her feel, even then, impotently angry that she hadn't been able to share or cushion his hurt. Suddenly she felt sixteen again, bewildered and afraid of the sensations evoked and her inability to govern them.

When she eventually raised her eyes, the thread of her argument had long since eluded her. His expression transfixed her; his eyes were filled with a blind, piercing hunger, pagan in its unsophisticated rawness and far removed from anything she'd imagined a human face could portray.

'I'll never submit to blackmail.'

She wanted to feel the contours of the sharply defined cheekbones beneath her fingers, trace the jawline, surrender to the erotic clamour of his compelling eyes. She gave a small cry filled with a hopelessness that suddenly swamped her. He was capable of carrying out any threat, which meant he'd inevitably discover the true state of her feelings. Ignoring the sound of her own name as he called her with an urgency that made no impact, she ran outdoors.

The horizon had a crystal clarity where all the shades of blue met in one glorious colour, obliterating the line between sky and sea. Emily stared at the panorama without actually seeing it; none of the azure shades had the same inspired depth as Luke's eyes.

'I'm not sixteen any more, Luke.' She didn't have to turn to be aware in every fibre of her being of the tall, silent figure who had followed her down to the lochside.

'I'd noticed the difference, Emily. I think maybe you've still got a four-year-old unresolved fantasy. Could be therapeutic if we worked it through.'

She took a deep, steadying breath and twisted around to look him full in the eyes. 'You seem a little slow on the uptake, Luke,' she sneered, her heart thudding. 'I'm not interested.'

His eyes were amazingly cold, a blue chill that went bone-deep. 'We both know that's not true,' he said clearly, each word enunciated with terrible clarity.

Combating a rising swell of frantic panic, she swung away, only to be caught by iron fingers and spun back. One

hand caught and cupped her chin, wrenching her head upwards. It was true and he could say it with no trace of
tenderness. She swallowed. God help me, do I want tenderness…from him? The knowledge appalled her.

'Don't turn your back on me,' he responded savagely. 'I
realise a gentleman,' he drawled the word mockingly,
'doesn't mention such obvious facts, but your indifference
has taken the form of a combination of petty aggression
and smouldering glances interspersed with the sort of tension that only comes when two people are a long way off
indifferent to one another.'

Her pupils expanded until the colour of her eyes was
almost totally obliterated. 'What are you implying?' she
responded shakily. Why had he had to say it, bring it out
into the open? Ignore it and it'll go away was out of the
question now.

'I'm not implying anything,' he said tersely, his tone
scornful. 'I'm observing that denying something makes it
no less real. The way I see it, just because our being together can be served up as the ultimate punishment for
Charlie, it doesn't alter the fact that it's what we both
want.'

'I'm in love with Gavin,' she protested, her voice shrill
and discordant in her ears. It was a lie. She had faced the
fact that she had never loved Gavin. Gavin had offered a
security without the involvement of strong emotional bonds,
and that had appealed to her. She had instinctively wanted
to avoid any situations fraught with the sort of unpredictable,
exhausting, exhilarating elements…exhilarating! 'What
you're suggesting makes a mockery of everything marriage
is based on. It's a purely temporary measure—two birds with
one stone. Once you've inflicted humiliation on my family
and lost interest in sleeping with me, a nice clean divorce,'
she said with disgust.

'Sleeping with you, Emily? I'm not interested in sleeping, though I've had precious little of that commodity recently.' She was aware of the deepened shadows beneath his eyes as she listened to his dry voice. 'What's been going on with us has been something more…' the low, vibrant throb of his voice was so hypnotic that a debilitating lassitude took a direct route to her limbs '…primitive.' She knew he must have felt the violent tremor that swept through her like a gust of wind.

The small derisive laugh was whisked away by a sudden flurry that swept in off the loch. 'I think you've become too involved with your fiction to see the rather more mundane realities of life clearly,' she continued, her voice containing a betraying quiver as her eyes watched him bend down and select a flat, dull pebble which he casually sent skipping over the water. His air of relaxation was an added injury to her floundering confusion. She was aware of the smooth ripple of muscles in his shoulder tautening against the fabric of his shirt, and the concentration that made his profile still as he delivered the throw.

'The way I see it, you've succeeded in a typically disreputable way to turn my misfortune to your advantage.' Her teeth connected with her lower lip as he dusted his hands on his jeans and turned directly to face her derision with the quirk of one dark brow. 'And don't start all that stuff about mutual advantage and the kindness of your heart,' she swiftly added. 'You planned this whole nightmare.'

'I didn't bind you and gag you to get you here,' he pointed out, pivoting on his heel until he faced her. 'You went along with it because deep down it's where you want to be…here with me.'

His arrogance was breathtaking. 'While the balance of my mind was disturbed, I think is the common phrase. I was kidnapped. In retrospect, I can see that hitching on the motorway would have been preferable.'

One corner of his mouth curled contemptuously and his eyebrows rose in patent disbelief.

'What's wrong, Emmy, have you decided against delivering a taste of his own medicine?'

Her brow furrowed in genuine confusion.

'Wasn't that part of what you had in mind, infant? Give the bastard a taste of his own medicine, see how he likes the idea of you in another man's bed? I rather thought you were experimenting with that idea.'

The concept he was casually outlining made her colour fluctuate wildly as she grasped his crude point with escalating fury. 'You think I had it in mind to sleep with you just to prove to Gavin I can be equally imprudent and promiscuous?' Her voice rose to an incredulous squeak. She was aware that his opinion of her was low...but this!

'You mean big sister wasn't the first?' Luke clicked his tongue in mock-sympathy.

'Don't judge the rest of humanity by your abysmally low standards.'

'Excuse me,' he drawled. 'But you did say promiscuous.'

'If you think I'd lower myself to score points off Gavin you are sadly mistaken,' she continued, gritting her teeth and ignoring his gibes. 'I realise you think you're totally irresistible, but I acquired immunity when I was sixteen. My bloodstream is positively crammed with antibodies that make me want to throw up at the idea of you...' Her mouth went dry as she met his lancet blue regard. What had possessed her to dredge up a piece of dusty history? she wondered bleakly.

'Undoing the buttons on your blouse?' he supplied helpfully as her tongue refused to curl around the words necessary to complete her sentence.

She froze as his fingers began to perform the task he described so matter-of-factly, a task so intimate that she had no experience with which to compare it. Had she actually married Gavin, this would have been his right, to remove her clothes and touch her flesh with a possessive certainty that he would please her, that it was his right. Could she ever have allowed him this and other greater intimacies?

Her tongue clave to the roof of her mouth as she watched Luke—his hands, to be precise...long, lean fingers—in a horrified fascination. Where was her instinctive fastidious distaste now? The one that had gripped her at the notion of Gavin doing what Luke was doing now with such casual expertise? She shook her head in a mute denial of what he was doing, what she was permitting. The heat was a solid thing in the pit of her belly. It rose until it occluded her windpipe, fogged her thought processes.

She had imagined this so many times that it had seemed real. Luke had spent more time than usual at Charlcot during her sixteenth summer. He'd been recovering from an injury he'd sustained during the coverage of a violent coup in a Third World country, a fact that had increased his glamour in her eyes. Only the age-gap had stopped him declaring his feelings, she was convinced. She had spent her time in a permanent daydream, awaiting the magical moment when she was sure he would be overcome by the passion that consumed him. Just the thought of him could make her body react to an imaginary touch. The power her mind had over her body had fascinated her. She'd constructed so many complex fantasies, placed herself in mortal danger from which he inevitably rescued her. Her eyes had followed him with transparent yearning. The thought of it made her curl up with embarrassment. What he had actually seen had been an awkward adolescent.

Now the fantasy was happening, but it had never been like this...a sweet, aching violation of body and will both intolerable and addictive. She was going to stop him— wasn't she? The soft, cool air against her skin passed unnoticed as Luke's hand cupped first one breast and then the other in his hand, his fingers sliding over the brief lacy covering. Sensations were building up layer upon layer, intermeshed, swelling the pleasure, the unacknowledged hunger.

Self-preservation was screeching in her head, but the hypnotic spell of sensual enchantment his voice and hands had spun held her immobile.

'You have blossomed a little since sixteen,' he mused slowly. Emily was too submerged in the chaotic jumble of unaccustomed craving to register the unsteadiness in the deep rhythm of his voice. She was blind to the raw hunger that flickered in his eyes. A white-hot fire smouldered at the back of his eyes. Her own eyelids prickled with hot, painful pin-pricks, and her head dropped back, exposing the slender column of her throat to his greedy gaze.

'Sixteen?' she echoed, wishing her mind would begin to function independently of her senses; they were saturated, and it hurt to feel so much when she knew she shouldn't.

One of his hands slid down her cap of silky, honey-coloured hair, capturing in his fist the strands at the nape of her neck. The other remained on her ribcage just below the swell of her breasts. 'The crush—don't you recall?'

They'd laughed when she'd walked in on them. The blonde had been older than he was...a friend of her mother's, prematurely widowed and enjoying the situation to the full. It had cured Emily instantly. She'd felt betrayed and disgusted, but relieved that her torrid fantasies had stayed firmly private in her head. It seemed Luke had a good deal of insight into these things. It wasn't by accident that Gavin had been the antithesis of Luke. The painful lesson had made her wary of the qualities he had which made him so fatally attractive. Gavin had been the safe option.

'You were speaking about antibodies?'

Emily felt life flow back into her limbs. She tore herself free of him. 'You disgust me,' she hissed, pulling the loose edges of her blouse together as his eyes strayed on the heaving contours of her breasts. This was all a lesson just to prove how irresistible Luke was; or did he need to humiliate her because she'd committed the ultimate sin—she was a Stapely?

'If I were going to teach Gavin a lesson I'd choose someone who didn't despise me because of who my father is. Dear God, Luke, you must think I'm stupid. You're so twisted you'd probably tape the event and post it to Dad,' she accused, disgust, aimed mostly at her own helpless response, and aching sound in her voice. 'I'm not a stupid teenager any more.' I might as well be. At least I kept an illusion of pride then, and then I didn't know how deep and deadly was Luke's need—need for retribution, she thought despairingly.

'At least you were honest then,' he interrupted, his voice as calm as her own was frantic. 'If I were so lost to any sense of morality, so single-minded, hasn't it occurred to you that I could have blighted the Stapely pride much more thoroughly simply by taking what you were so eager to offer at the time?'

'You were distracted by the merry widow, that's all,' she sneered. 'Providence cured me and saved me from making an even bigger fool of myself. Or you just couldn't stomach the thought of touching a Stapely.'

Luke made a scornful noise. 'Didn't you ever realise that that little scene was stage-managed with the precise intention of curing you of the infatuation? It's a tricky situation for a man in his twenties to be worshipped by a girl in the grip of pubescent hormonal imbalance. It was either that or do what you were so anxious for. I think the reality would have sent you running even faster. I don't think you were as ready for the grown-up league as you thought.'

Had that been his idea of kindness? The cruel reminder of her naïve transparency made her flush. 'You expect me to believe that,' she snorted, 'after I've seen how much you hate my parents? You could have ruined me.' Why wouldn't he have? Was she to believe in scruples after she had glimpsed the indelible hate in his eyes, knew what his plans for her future were?

Silently he looked into her eyes, his expression at its most impenetrable. 'Naturally you feel I wouldn't have passed up the opportunity.' He half turned away, his expression one of distaste. 'At that time I half thought there might be something worth protecting, nurturing, in those big, transparent brown eyes. Even though you were a spoilt brat I thought by some miracle you'd been spared the taint.' He gave a mirthless laugh and continued with heavy irony, 'I had no way of seeing what a deceitful apology for a woman you'd turn into. But then, when it comes down to it you are a Stapely. You're as shallow and self-serving as the rest of them,' he said with thin-lipped distaste.

She took a step backwards as though he'd struck her. 'You are the arbiter of taste in womanly attributes, I take it.' Her voice was hard but inside for some reason she wanted to cry, weep like the child she no longer was. Mentally she remonstrated with herself for this wrenching, instinctive response to his cold indictment.

'If homogenised life is what you want, far be it from me to criticise.'

His drawl made her want to run at him, fists flying. 'Look at me, will you?' she snapped, catching hold of his sleeve, aware even in the heat of the moment of the sinewy hardness beneath the fabric. 'You *were* criticising…you *are*. Who gave you the right?' she demanded fiercely.

'Why in God's name did you never break free?' The words erupted and the anger in his face was savage. 'After university, you went back to that bloody mausoleum. Haven't you got any backbone? I expected more—much more of you. I thought I saw some integrity in your eyes once.'

The unexpectedness of the accusation, and the accompanying information that Luke had spared a passing thought for her, made her catch her breath. 'Terribly sorry to be such a profound disappointment to you,' she snapped with heavy irony, quashing the unexpected sense of guilt as though she had to justify herself to him.

'What is the great attraction of Charlcot? The company of sweet little Charlotte? That's the same poor soul who swiped your boyfriend, is it?' he asked with a quirk of one eyebrow. 'Dear Charlotte, beneath her wistful-little-girl looks, can manage very nicely, thank you. What had you intended to do, take her with you when you got hitched? As things have turned out I'm sure hubby would have been amenable. I mean, two of you might have doubled his promotion prospects!'

So the only thing that would make a man want her was her family's wealth, was it? She saw his face distorted through a glaze of tears. 'You are a pig. I don't see what it is about my life that offends you so much.'

'I hate waste.' The sudden flash in his eyes made her blink, and she struggled against the hands that turned and caught her own forearms, half dragging her towards him. 'Your life is aseptically neat, down to the last ingredient— a lover you can control and never be out of control with. You can't even be honest about what the guy actually meant to you. All this tearful carping about loving him. I know honest emotion doesn't exist in the precincts of Charlcot's palatial walls, but you can't invent life to suit your own purposes. You have to get out, get bruised, sample things, *live*. You can't plan life; it just happens if you let it.'

'You complacent, smug…' She twisted wildly, infuriated by the denunciation of her life. 'You've done all those things, I take it. I should possibly follow your example. The first step is naturally to walk, blessing my good fortune, into your bed—and leave a better and wiser person! Like the multitude that have been there before me!' She almost choked on the sentence. 'Did you have to blackmail them too? I know you for what you are, Lucas Hunt, and I know you don't give a damn about me or how I feel. I'm just a way to get back at my parents, a tool. Well, for your information I like them as little as you do. I have never looked to a soul-mate to live my life through—I've seen poor Charlotte try and do that. I might have made a mistake where Gavin was concerned, but at least I wasn't blinded by some animal lust elevated for the sake of convention to the heights of some sickly romantic ideal. I don't intend to start bed-hopping now!' A sudden sob, dry and racking, robbed her of words. 'From your point of view I'm a failure. Think what a lot that gives you in common with my parents.' She held her hands up to fend off his attempt to recapture her. Whether this physical approach was meant to comfort or censure she had no notion.

'You can hardly accuse me of advocating casual relationships, Emily, not when it's marriage I'm proposing.' His eyes were almost navy with emotion, turbulent and as angry as she'd ever seen him. 'As for getting you in my bed, my taste runs to warm, confident women who don't need reassurance every other word. When did you become such a soulless little cynic, Emily? You'll marry me because you're afraid of what it will do to your father if he believes we were lovers four years ago. When it boils down to it, you know that despite all the window-dressing and protests you're still the dutiful little girl,' he said derisively. 'You can be as sanctimonious as you like, rant on about the lust you clearly expect me to believe you find distasteful, but the truth, Emily, is you can't cope with your own sexuality. You want to be that little girl,' he told her, his mouth compressed to an austere line of distaste. 'You don't hate the way my mouth feels on yours; you're hungry to taste me.' He made a guttural sound in his throat and released her hands. 'You're aching for me to touch you,' he continued with blighting scorn. 'But if it makes you happy in your own perverse way to think you're nothing but an unwilling victim, fine.' He shrugged.

'I don't know what you mean,' she faltered.

'Has it occurred to you, infant, that the sacrifice is mine? Marrying a Stapely is hardly my life's ambition. Nothing matters to me except repaying a debt. It makes the slate clean as far as I'm concerned.'

'Is that supposed to be some sort of incentive to go along with this crazy scheme?' The fact that she loved him gave him a unique ability to inflict a staggering amount of pain... The only redeeming factor was that that, at least, remained her own secret. 'If I marry you, Luke, to stop you telling Dad all those vindictive lies, it will be a marriage in name only. Considering I'm the unclean, a full-blooded Stapely, you can hardly object to those terms.'

He regarded her with an absence of emotion that was bedrock, cold. 'I'll need to get a valid licence once we get back to London...that will be long enough for you to re-think that scheme, Emily.'

'I won't—' she began hotly.

'And when you do,' he interrupted, a small, malicious smile playing about his lips, 'you'll do the asking!' He strode away from her without a backward glance, his spine rigidly erect, his long legs putting distance between them swiftly.

'Never, never, never...' she muttered to herself from between clenched teeth.

CHAPTER SIX

'DO YOU PLAN to work so industriously all evening, or will you join me to eat? This is by way of being a celebratory meal,' Luke reminded her mockingly.

Emily had stiffened the moment he'd leant over her to see the typewritten words on the page she'd been transcribing. 'I've no doubt you would consider it a celebration,' she replied coldly. He had her tacit agreement to this farcical marriage, his ultimate revenge; he couldn't make her act as though she was happy about the situation! For years he'd waited for such an opportunity, and she had provided it.

'And such a diligent fianceé—I scarcely need secretarial assistance.'

Emily flexed her stiff neck. 'There's precious little else to do here,' she muttered. The truth was that occupying her hands if not her thoughts had been one way of avoiding him; the cottage was too small actually to escape. Eventually she had even begun to be engrossed by the story unfolding beneath her fingertips. Luke's storylines were always original, and underlying the brisk action was a depth of local knowledge, no doubt gleaned from his extensive travels. It was the underlying vulnerability of the hero which had captured her interest, because beneath the gung-ho exterior he was a man attempting to regain an idealism she knew his inventor to despise.

She flinched as Luke's long fingers began to knead the tight muscles of her shoulders and neck through the thin

material of her shirt. Magically he was locating and elim-
inating knots of tension. It was a dangerously pleasant feeling, one which made her feel languidly relaxed. His next
words made her realise what a dangerous condition that was
to be in.

'I can think of other activities to which you could apply
your feverish energy,' he drawled, and she choked on the
sigh of pleasure that had been leaving her lips, instantly
alert to the danger of his fingers and the seductive, gravelly
drawl of his voice.

'I was just trying to relieve the monotony of your constant company,' she responded, standing up and distancing
herself from him. 'If you've cooked I might as well sample
what you have to offer. And there's no need to leer in that
vulgar manner,' she grated. 'It's the food I'm referring to.'
His expression could in no way be classified as a leer, but
it was incredibly disruptive, a fact her trembling limbs bore
witness to as she followed him through to the dining area.

'I do enjoy a smattering of vulgarity myself, infant, but
then I'm not a Stapely, am I?' he said, holding a chair for
her with mock-formality. 'Actually I wasn't offering anything but food. We must keep up your strength.'

Emily glared at him, managing with effort to retain her
self-control. 'For the ordeal ahead.'

'Wedding nerves,' he observed sympathetically. He only
grinned wryly as she ignored him and took the other seat
on the opposite side of the table. 'A common affliction.'
He moved to the kitchen area and began to dispense a very
passable spaghetti sauce. 'Aren't you glad I'm a modern
man? I can cook, wash, sew on buttons...'

'The perfect wife,' she snapped nastily. 'Don't forget
blackmail. Your talents are impressive—I'm still congrat-
ulating myself on my supreme good fortune.' She almost
choked on the sense of injustice that swelled in her chest.

'I have hidden depths,' he agreed, with a smug indifference to her distress that made her want to scream.

'So do sewers!'

Luke placed a heaped plate in front of her. 'Be careful, infant, or I might think you're trying to be grotesquely offensive. Parmesan?' he asked, as she opened her mouth to confirm this accusation vehemently. 'And I might have to take measures to break that little habit early on in our relationship.'

Emily took the cheese and glowered at him as he took his seat opposite her. 'I may be going to marry you, Luke, but, believe you me, I won't be the sort of wife you'll want your friends to meet. You'd be amazed at how indiscreet I can be when I put my mind to it!' she warned him. She wanted to make it clear that his intimidatory tactics left her unimpressed.

'That should win me the sympathy vote, if nothing else,' he said drily.

Discretion won the day after a brief internal battle, and their conversation stayed safely monosyllabic. The food was good and Emily realised just how hungry she was as she attacked it. The wine eventually dulled the edge of her anger and thawed some of her open hostility.

'Do you write for yourself or to sell books?' The words came out gruffly to break one of the long silences that had arisen. Not companionable silences, at least not on her part, but noisy silences when her mind grew over-active and her motor skills stiff and awkward.

Luke looked up from his task of mopping up the glass of wine she'd tipped over the table. 'What was that, Emily?' he asked, and she had the impression that he'd only been half listening to her. His mind was obviously elsewhere, she thought resentfully. She repeated her question with a hint of hauteur this time.

He straightened up and rolled the cuffs of his shirt up his forearms, exposing the dark, tanned skin covered with a fine mesh of dark hair. 'Are you getting very intense and asking me about artistic integrity?' he asked in the lazy, mocking way she was accustomed to. 'Actually I'm in the fortunate position of being able to do both without having to compromise too much.' He raised a brow as she refilled her empty glass. 'Is that wise, considering the present state of your co-ordination?'

Emily narrowed her eyes. 'Do I need your permission?'

'You can get plastered and swing from the chandeliers as far as I'm concerned, infant,' he replied, his light tone at variance with her swift antagonism.

'I think I can guarantee I won't do that,' she returned, colour tingeing her cheekbones. 'I thought authors based their heroes on themselves? Yours are always so… ordinary.'

'Aren't I?'

The cerulean blue of his eyes was intent and difficult to look away from. His overt male vitality jarred on her senses; the only predictable thing about Luke, she found herself thinking, was that he would always be unpredictable. Ordinary he would never be.

'You call managing to juggle a career as a photo-journalist with news reporting and writing very ordinary?' she drawled nastily, as though this excess of talent were a criminal activity.

He shrugged. 'And lots of women hold down a job, rear children and run a home. What's so special? I can be selfish. I have no one to please but myself, so I do.'

'But what do you think of yourself as?' she persisted, realising this modesty was totally genuine and feeling shock: it was out of tune with all her notions of him. She'd so often heard him referred to at home as arrogant, self-important, that the scathing denunciations had gradually seeped into her mental filing system as truth. How many of her concepts about Luke were culled second-hand? she wondered. Was she as guilty of prejudice as he?

'Why this desperate need to pigeon-hole, infant?' He held his glass at arm's length and watched her narrow-eyed through the deep red liquid, twirling the stem between his fingers. 'I mean, I have no ambition to write the definitive book, so I don't fear dilution of my talent. Opportunities arise and I take them. It always seemed churlish not to. I've been lucky—in the right place at the right time,' he mused. 'It would be terrible to wonder what might have been—so much easier to find out.' He made it sound so damned easy, she thought resentfully. 'People are just people,' he continued reflectively. 'It's the way they react in extraordinary circumstances that makes them different; that's why people can relate to my characters.' He made a dismissive gesture and took a swallow of his wine. 'At least, that's what my agent says.'

'Luke, how long do you intend staying here?'

The faint smile that had hovered around his lips deepened, etching lines from his nose to the corners of his mouth. Humour evaporated, leaving an impatient edge of anger. 'Tired of my company so soon?'

'It's so claustrophobic here...I can't breathe!' The words exploded from her. Aware that the blast of emotion had made him stare with frightening intensity, she toyed with the top button of her shirt, unconsciously drawing the attention of his deep blue brooding stare to her throat.

'Miles of open space...claustrophobic?' She met his taunting stare with an expression of deep frustration. 'Or is it I that fills you with the desire to escape?' he said with accurate perception.

'I just want to get this farce over with and reconstruct my life. I'm not multi-talented like you, but I think I could be a good teacher. If I had some idea of the time-span you had envisaged as a suitable punishment for Dad without interfering with your life too much, I could plan for the future.' She half envied the pragmatism of the person speaking; it certainly had nothing to do with the churning mass of uncertainty which had converted her thought processes to a basic survival mode.

A spark of something that was instantly subdued shone briefly in his eyes. 'They didn't want you to teach, did they?' His fixed stare from beneath half-closed eyelids was not as casual as his tone.

'I was supposed to be a social asset and a professional shopper, like Charlotte,' she snapped, and felt ashamed at the implied criticism of her sister—though in the circumstances, she thought wryly, Charlotte had earned a little criticism. 'But I showed little talent in that direction. You know Dad; his opinion of female intellect is no secret. The most stupid male is still inherently superior to a female, even if she just happens to have won a Pulitzer.'

Luke nodded reflectively. 'You still did what you wanted in the end. I take it Gavin wasn't encouraging you to pursue your career? You just trotted obediently back home and got auctioned off to the highest bidder. If the home had been any other, quite understandable...'

'Anything for a quiet life,' she replied flippantly.

'Why?' he persisted.

'I like Charlcot,' she lied fluently. 'I could never have afforded anywhere so palatial.' She wasn't going to elaborate on her father's drastic tactics, the heartless scheme she had so stupidly fallen for. Luke never accepted anything at face value; he'd think her a total fool for doing so. She discovered she had no wish further to reinforce his poor opinion of her father, however accurate it might be. For some obscure reason she felt strangely responsible for every indictment he brought against them, as though she were personally responsible. He acted as though she were, she thought bleakly.

'I don't believe that.'

'Your privilege.' She shrugged. 'Anyway, I still want to know when I can get back to civilisation.'

'A sensitive soul might infer that my company doesn't please you. Or are you anxious to embark on a spell of marital bliss?' His grin broadened, very white in his tanned face. 'Or could it be that you just don't trust yourself to resist the carnal interest that's stirring in your delectable breast? There's an interesting thought.'

'Is that supposed to be a joke?' she asked rigidly.

He tilted his head and his expression sobered, became brooding and ambiguous. His lips, miraculously sensual enough to make the muscles in her belly tighten, curved cynically. 'Not necessarily, as you're well aware,' he grated. 'I made myself clear earlier, I think. Which simplifies matters, infant. Now you only have to worry about your own instincts,' he coldly reminded her of his parting shot.

The blood singing in her ears made her vision blur. 'Let me go, Luke.' The appeal, the panic, were clear in each syllable. How easy it was for him to send her spiralling out of control; how he must be laughing, she thought, bitterly angry at her inability to carry off the situation. His eyes weren't laughing, though, when she blinked to clear her vision and his lean frame seemed taut with the same tension that was making her tremble. 'Forget this whole stupid idea. Dad would never believe we slept together... I was just a child.'

'Sixteen is no child, at least not for the purposes we're dealing with. And I am the Antichrist in your family's eyes, capable of any infamy.' He gave a hard laugh. 'In your eyes too,' he added with biting irony. 'I think I'm capable of convincing Charlie that you were a very willing victim, Emmy, and you know it.'

He had her cornered and he knew it. 'Don't do that,' she pleaded huskily as he steepled his fingers and allowed his intense stare to rest unblinkingly on her face.

'What?'

'Look at me like...that.' He was being so cruel, and yet he could make her ache with unfulfilled desire, a consuming yearning. She felt the blood run hot beneath her skin as she shivered in helpless response.

'You're a beautiful woman; I would have thought you could take it in your stride by now.'

'Am I supposed to be flattered by that comment?' she asked derisively. 'I can see you think of me as some sort of trophy.' Nothing else, unfortunately, explained his persistence. She despised herself for wistfully imagining what it would be like if his motivations were not inspired by vengeance. 'A Stapely, a notch on the bed-post. You're an attractive man and my ego has taken a battering, but I'm not stupid enough to be a willing pawn in your sick game. If you wait for me to do the asking, you'll wait forever,' she gasped huskily.

She wanted to make him angry, but not angry enough to push the issue. Her voice sounded cold, like the sweat that bathed her body. She couldn't let him know how easily she could succumb to the love which drew her to him despite the objections of the small, still sane portion of her brain. A portion that he could make mute with a single touch... He couldn't know. *She* knew, though, and despised herself for this fatal weakness.

'Get a kick from self-denial, do you, Em?' His derision was apparent. His whole attitude betrayed the fact that he had no appetite for self-denial himself.

Why had she never seen past the sleek, urbane exterior and realised earlier the danger he represented? Here was a man who could dodge shell-fire and not by so much as a blink give away the fact that he wasn't comfortably seated in a studio. The toughness, the determination went bone-deep, as did the cynicism. The nature of his role in the media meant that he was constantly bombarded with the very worst of human suffering and inhumanity. He'd told her he had seen wickedness and felt nothing, a spiritual numbness she couldn't believe, having read his work a few hours earlier. Through the words ran a surprising thread of idealism that shone through at unexpected moments from the corrosive cynicism, as if the two fought a constant battle.

The blue eyes were anything but passive at the moment. She found her stomach doing painful contortions as she met his gaze. 'I'm all for anticipation, prolonging the relish, but you can take that too far.'

'How many times do I have to say it, Luke? I don't want to sleep with you!' she cried, defying the deep instinct to reach out, be submerged by the fleeting passion he felt, and forget that he only despised her. Hadn't he told her as much? She was helpless to prevent the electrical surge that began as a gentle tingling beneath her skin, and grew, exploded into arrows of molten pain...desire. She tried to think past the demands of her body; even without the feud things were hopeless; their lives were poles apart. 'I'm particular about whom I make love with, and to be quite frank I find all of this quite sordid,' she said frigidly, and beneath the table her knees shook.

'Sordid?' Soft and purring, his tone spelt danger. Luke was angry; in fact he was furious. She could see the thin white bloodless line that outlined his compressed lips. A nerve leapt erratically in his lean cheek, and his eyes shot blue wrath.

'We're related,' she responded, feeling cornered by the disproportionate response.

His eyebrows rose sarcastically. 'Our parents were cousins only because my mother was adopted. We are related on paper, not by blood. I think you can rule out incest in whatever culture you care to align yourself with.'

'This is pointless,' she muttered, rising. 'I don't have to have a note to excuse me just because I don't want to go to bed with you. You might blackmail me into marriage, but I'll despise you with all my heart.' She gave a muttered expletive as her sleeve caught the coffee-pot, disgorging the contents over her hand. The pain helped her concentrate her wits. 'Don't touch me!' she yelped shrilly as he made a move towards her. One step nearer, and a word of concern, and she'd be lost...

'You should do something about that hand,' Luke said after a pause.

She felt oddly deflated that he had obeyed her fierce command so readily. 'I'm quite capable of doing so if necessary.'

'I wasn't offering any assistance,' he said without expression. 'And, Emmy,' he said as she turned to escape. She looked back over her shoulder warily. 'You do want to be in my bed.'

She made a faint choking noise in her throat.

He didn't follow her; that much at least she should have been thankful for. The irony was, half of her had longed for him to do just that. That was too easy, though... She had to capitulate. Her submission had to be total—part of the retribution!

Placing her raw hand underneath the running water did nothing to relieve the burning sensation that ran like molten liquid through her body. Such wanting, such despair...she had never dreamt that such terrible depths existed. Sadly mourning her lost innocence, she closeted herself in the small dressing-room. Was the chest of drawers she pushed up against the door to keep him out or herself in? she wondered bleakly as she climbed into the narrow bed.

THE NIGHTMARE reappeared and she emerged from the visceral terror slick with sweat, whimpers still escaping from a throat raw from the terrified screams that had split the night.

The sound of splintering wood and the thud of the overturned chest only added to her confusion. She blinked as light from the room beyond, Luke's room, flooded into her own small ante-room.

Luke's eyes took in the overturned furniture and her white-faced figure, eyes huge, tears still running down her cheeks. 'Furniture removal, infant?' he observed, but the erratic throb of the nerve in his jaw belied the dry tone. 'Rape,' he said derisively, 'was never on the agenda.'

She couldn't counter his anger; she was still shaking. 'N-night terrors,' she stammered. 'I hardly ever get them now.' She gripped the bedcover and pleated it between her trembling fingers. 'I expect I was yelling.'

'My name.'

She closed her eyes. The terror which had been so stark wasn't as severe as the apprehension which assailed her now. Yelling out for him like some lovesick idiot... You're nothing to him but a dupe, Emily... If you're going to be used, girl, retain a little dignity! It was difficult to keep her mind running along these lines when it wanted to make detours concerning the way the line of hair on his chest disappeared into the pair of shorts he wore, the muscular contractions in his belly and thighs that made the skin glide like well-oiled teak over the compact conformation.

'Sorry I disturbed you.' In the circumstances she was pleased with the way it sounded. At least it had been articulate, not a hysterical scream!

'Disturbed? What a way you have with words, infant,' he drawled. He spoke after a pause that had been so heavy with unspoken comment that her reluctant eyes had been forced open.

'Luke...'

'Do you honestly believe it's worth fighting against the tide of something that's inevitable, Emily?' he asked harshly, his blue eyes banked with smouldering embers.

She took a deep breath. What had she been waiting for, some declaration of love? How stupid, she derided herself. It had been something in his eyes that for one brief moment had made her hopes flare. 'I haven't your dedication and single-minded ambition, Luke. I don't get a sadistic kick from gaining the upper hand, and neither do I polish my grudges over the years,' she informed him, shivering as the dampness on her skin grew cold and clammy. 'The only inevitable thing I know is how much I'm going to despise you. Marriage to you is still a nightmare, not a reality.'

His shadowed jaw grew taut and the air of restrained violence in his body grew more pronounced. With a single violent epithet he stalked, panther-like, to her narrow bed.

'What are you doing...?' she squeaked.

'You have a habit of asking questions with answers which are painfully obvious to anyone but a complete imbecile,' he growled, adjusting the angle of his jaw as a strand of her hair snaked around his neck. He glared at her, his manner one of intense exasperation. 'I'm taking you to my bed and, before you start to make speeches about my sullying your integrity just by occupying the same planet, I will go to great lengths to assure you that the only reason for this is I haven't the energy to break down any more doors to rescue you.'

'I don't need rescuing.' The curve of his shoulder was so inviting that it took all her will-power to hold herself stiffly rigid in his arms as he carried her into his room.

'If you don't shut up, you will,' he promised grimly. Without warning she landed on his bed, an undignified tangle of arms and legs.

'I can't sleep here!' She pulled her nightdress down over her knees with unsteady fingers.

'Sweetheart, I've indulged you to the hilt so far,' he said on a note of warning.

'Not so as you'd notice,' she retorted, outraged enough by this patently untrue statement to protest. He really was a barbarian—the word seemed disturbingly apt. He was standing in a diminishing circle of light which faded away to shadow at the perimeter of the room. The shadow playing across his skin lent it a satin-like bronze glow. The sharp planes of his face were illuminated, giving the contours an austere, almost sinister beauty. She tore her eyes away from him. To her, he symbolised the essence of raw, earthy masculinity. The effect it had on her made her appreciate how wildly optimistic she'd been in imagining she could keep her secret.

'I need sleep, so why make a drama out of sharing a bed? I've already told you, Emmy, that the initiative is yours, sweetheart. I'm prepared to be seduced if your offer is good enough.'

The air whistled through her clenched teeth. Of all the arrogant... A shudder ran through her as he threw back the quilt and slid beneath it. He raised himself and regarded her, dark brows drawn together in a line of disdain. 'I want you where I know you can come to no harm.'

'Sharing your bed is not my idea of security!' The fact that the heat from his body had already invaded the small space that separated them, that all she had to do was reach out, made her skin prickle as though subjected to a constant, ruthless friction.

He slid down. 'Just think how convenient it will be if you have any more erotic dreams,' he told her, leaning over to flick off the bedside lamp.

'Nightmares,' she hissed.

'Erotic nightmares,' he obliged. 'Goodnight, Emmy.' He rolled on to his side, his breathing quickly becoming deep and regular.

She lay stiff and miserable at his side. The whole situation put things alarmingly into perspective. The sort of longing which was attacking every atom of her being was searing...agonising. Yet Luke could calmly fall asleep! Any desire he felt for her had been incited by his ruthless determination to flaunt their liaison under her father's nose; it was pointless for her to elevate it to anything more worthy.

Eventually she must have slept, and surprisingly she was troubled by none of the recent turbulent dreams. Consciousness returned slowly, a warm, drifting sensation she reluctantly permitted herself to obey. Light. Sleepily her eyes focused on a wooden beam above her head. She tried to roll over and gave a puzzled, sleepy frown as a dead weight restricted her movements.

Reality swiftly replaced the hazy sense of well-being. Her eyes darted around the alien room and confirmed she'd had no right to indulge in optimism. The dead weight was Luke's arm, and the warmth was the length of his body. Stifling panic, she twisted on to her side and pulled herself free of his arm. Desperate not to disturb him, she lay listening for any sign of returning consciousness in him. Feeling safer as he continued to lie supine and unmoving, she slid her legs towards the edge of the bed. At this point she permitted herself a covert glance towards his sleeping figure. Asleep, Luke's face had lost the ingrained cynicism. He looked younger and, if not quite vulnerable, certainly less remote. With a will of their own her eyes moved covetously lower.

The impact made her gasp, the sound the only audible noise in the room. Clothes had not hidden the sleek strength of his body, but they had blurred the details. In the morning light what had been the suggestion of power was breathtakingly explicit. The densely packed muscles were more defined than she had imagined and, yes, she admitted, she *had* imagined! This was no boy's body; the raw masculine power hit some exposed area of her brain like a bolt of neat electricity. She stared dry-mouthed at the dark, curling hair scattered across the breadth of his chest, tailing to a narrow dart where it disappeared beneath the waistband of his boxer-shorts. His thighs were covered with the same fine dusting—strong, deeply muscled, athletic legs.

The effort not to touch him made her feel physically ill. Inside she began to experience a self-revulsion at the erotic images she couldn't extinguish. Images full of tactile sensations, sensations she felt desperate to experience. Her head felt incredibly light and she knew her flesh was burning; she felt branded by the heightened awareness.

'Did you sleep?'

Dazed, her eyes flickered back to his face. How long had he been awake, watching her? Guilt and self-disgust filtered into her eyes. How could she permit him to do this to her? She was a tool...a means of achieving his ultimate revenge...

She had to say something; he was watching her with that impenetrable stare. 'You have a nice tan.' She curled up inside as the fatuous words came blurting out and she steeled herself for the facetious response he would undoubtedly deliver.

Lazily he stretched. The muscles in her jaw felt tight enough to snap as she watched his muscles bunch and relax as he sat up in one fluid motion. His air of relaxation only deepened her horror at the feelings which writhed hungrily in the pit of her stomach.

'Seychelles, remember?'

'What were you doing there?' Her interest could be described as marginal, but she was making a supreme effort to disguise the fact that her eyes kept straying to the expanse of evenly tanned flesh.

'I was interviewing Bernie Cavanaugh for a Sunday supplement spread,' he announced, rubbing the stubble that shadowed his jaw.

Even at that moment, barely able to string two words together, she was impressed. 'The sculptor?'

Luke nodded. 'You know the work?'

'I've only seen it second-hand. How did you manage that, Luke? I thought he was a recluse. No one has set eyes on him for years.'

'It's a coup, as they say; and he's a she... Bernice.'

'Oh.'

'What exactly is that supposed to indicate?' The blue gaze was alarmingly speculative.

The amount of petulance and innuendo she had unwittingly slipped into the monosyllable was depressing.

Jealousy, she admitted, wondering what aberrant behaviour she would exhibit next. 'How did you persuade her to allow you to interview her?' she asked hurriedly. 'I suppose she must be quite old by now,' she added. The thought was somehow cheering.

His expression grew sardonic and his lips twisted into a crooked smile. 'Age, infant, is relative; and Bernice is one of the warmest, most open people I've come across. Serene is too placid a word to describe her, but she is comfortable with her own femininity without feeling the need to exploit it,' he reflected. 'As for persuading her, she saw a spread I did in *Time* last year and approached me.'

Emily's expression had grown sour as he'd described this talented paragon. 'I'm amazed you dragged yourself away.'

A strange expression flitted into Luke's eyes. 'I'm still not sure I should have,' he said grimly.

In the time it took her to register the sudden husky intonation and the restless flicker of unrefined hunger flare and subside in his expression, she realised he wasn't as relaxed as she had imagined. Intellectually he'd been able to support a pretence of normality, but the brief window had made her aware of the sinews pulled tightly in his neck, the air of restraint about him as if he was angrily confining some strong emotion which she was too afraid to analyse.

In a tangle of limbs she jumped off the bed. In the circumstances, conducting a conversation in this setting had not been one of her best moves. 'I need...' she began, her heart pounding furiously. As she met the angry smoulder of his eyes, her voice faded momentarily.

'Go on, Emily, this should prove interesting,' he encouraged. 'What do you need?'

His scornful drawl broke her free of the catatonic state. 'A cup of tea,' she told him stoically.

He pinned her with his slitted raw gaze. 'An original euphemism, Emily.' One brow rose, coolly sardonic, and she flushed madly. His sensuous mouth remained immobile as he watched the warm carnation flood her face. 'If you are prepared to marry me to save your father from the pain of knowing I knew his little girl in the biblical sense.'

'You didn't.'

'He wouldn't know that,' he pointed out heartlessly. 'If you are prepared to make the supreme sacrifice.'

'My father has a bad heart.' It was true, even if it wasn't as critical as she had been led to believe.

'The fact Charlie has a heart at *all* is news to me.'

'You're the heartless one,' she accused, her voice filled with loathing. 'Marriage isn't meant to be a means of retribution.'

'It's so sacred that you were going to marry Gavin with no deeper motivation than choosing a new duvet cover, he co-ordinated so well,' he said, the caressing sneer in his voice breaking new ground in insults. 'As I was saying,' he continued softly, 'I find your attitude difficult to fathom. You're prepared to be the dutiful daughter, but when it comes to accepting the benefits of our relationship you lie through your teeth. The fact is you can't think about anything much except touching me, being touched... You respond physically to me so dramatically—'

'Stop it!' she interrupted, holding up her hands in a defensive gesture as if to fend off his low, intimate purr that made her breasts ache and the muscles in her belly coil. 'As far as I'm concerned, you're the lowest form of humanity, a blackmailer...you make my skin crawl with revulsion. Anything else is conjured up by your imagination.' She met the incandescent flare of blue as their eyes collided, and the ambivalent expression of disgust and craving in his face so precisely mirrored what she was experiencing that she gave a small cry of instinctive fear and took to her heels, regardless of the fact that she was wearing only a short nightdress.

He caught up with her on the foreshore where her impetuous withdrawal had led her. 'Leave me alone!' she yelled as he approached.

Luke stopped several feet away, and his eyes swept disparagingly over her, making her aware of the ridiculous picture she must present—barefooted and clutching the light, knee-length nightdress that the wind had plastered to her body like a second skin. He, she saw, had paused to pull on a pair of trainers and jeans; his torso was still bare and his presence evoked the now almost familiar suffocating sensations.

His voice was hard with derisive contempt. 'That might prove difficult, if I wake up to find you dining on me with those, big, beautiful eyes.'

'A girl can look without necessarily being inspired to do anything else.' There was little point in denying the incident so fresh in her mind. She felt mortification stiffen her spine and make her face grow blank.

'That's true, no doubt…in some instances.'

She threw back her head at a haughty angle and pursued a bored expression with variable success. The face was easy to arrange but she couldn't wipe the fearful shadow from the cloudy golden depths. 'If it means so much to you, I'll go along with the pretence that I'm a slave to your masculine charms. I admit you're beautiful.' Some of the sarcasm evaporated from her voice at the wrong moment and she sounded so fervent that she hurried on, almost falling over her words to cover the emotions that had slipped through her guard. 'But, between ourselves, life would be a lot simpler if you stopped belabouring the point. I mean, the only reason you want me is to torture Dad—and he already believes this fantasy, or he will do once you've had a few minutes to enlighten him. So why bother? I mean, why contaminate yourself with my bloodline, not to mention all my neurotic inadequacies?'

'You could have a point there,' he said unsmilingly.

The reply deflated her, but she knew when to take advantage of a situation. She muttered a defiant, 'Fine,' and turned to go. She had barely taken two steps before a hand grabbed her arm and spun her around, almost jerking her off her feet as he catapulted her into his body.

'I'll tell you when to go,' he said thickly, and the tension in him communicated itself to her immediately. She stopped struggling and froze, sensing danger, excited by it despite the heart-thudding fear that flooded through her. He caught her chin in one hand and she couldn't prevent him forcing her face up to his.

'What do you think you're doing?' she asked shakily. His eyes scanning her face were incandescent, alight with a blatant hunger that was intensely shocking.

'Perhaps I'm prepared to risk contamination; it might just vindicate all the bloody aggravation of putting up with your continual whining, constant dissimulation!'

Had she ever thought him bland, urbane? He looked capable of just about anything right now. He was in the grip of some violent emotion which obviously was temporarily overriding his habitual control. She'd seen Luke maintain his legendary cool under severe provocation from her father, even under bullet fire. Yet she had pushed him right to the edge. 'I've told you before, I won't be a pawn to be sacrificed,' she said tremulously. 'I thought I had to beg the great Luke Hunt,' she reminded him.

His teeth grated audibly and the pallor around his lips deepened. 'You persist in acting as though you're just an interested observer. It would take me seconds to make you beg, less to make you admit you want me as badly as I want you.' Her stomach lurched at his violent admission, and she swayed as though struck by a strong wind. 'If it weren't for the fact of who I am, you'd still be in bed now…with me. Next you'll be telling me you've taken some vow of chastity,' he sneered, and his eyes darkened at the small bubble of hysterical laughter that overflowed from her constricted throat. 'Gavin can hardly have been the first to sample your sweet temptations—' His voice slurred slightly, and he broke off, sweat beading his forehead.

The image his words conjured up made her skin grow hot. She pressed damp palms flat against his chest and tried to push free. Her head snapped from side to side until the grip of his fingers tightened, holding her immobile. His thumb pushed back a strand of hair from her cheek. 'I don't meet the social criteria for a Stapely, do I, Emily? That's the problem. That's why you'll always choose some guy like Gavin who won't mess your hair in public or ruin Daddy's efforts to work his way to the top of the honours list. You're a hypocrite, born and bred,' he continued. 'Have you given many men the hungry, come-get-me look and then run away? The odds were that someone, sometime, would call your bluff, infant, and give you what you're drooling for. I should have known better. Away from the bloody tribe I thought you might...' If she'd looked up at that moment she might have glimpsed a bleak emptiness, an anguish that went deep.

She did raise her tear-filled eyes when his grip relaxed as he shook his head, regarding her with an expression that seemed to border on loathing. She took advantage of the moment and turned to flee once more, his scathing comments echoing in her ears. She ignored the sound of her name as he yelled after her, and ran. Actually, floundered would have been more accurate; the ground was pebbly and uneven, shelving sharply where it fell to the waterline, and her bare feet objected to such rough treatment. It was by luck rather than good management that her impetuous flight took her a hundred metres or so before the ground shifted beneath her feet and she slithered and fell.

The cold water took her breath away and she found herself sliding beneath the waist-deep, softly lapping waves. She surfaced and sank once more before she was able to get her footing.

He was standing there on the shore, watching her attempts to brush sea-water-sodden strands of hair from her eyes. His face was impassive.

'Go away!' she yelled, banging the water with her hand and sending a showering his direction. It was futile, childish, but she was past caring about minor details.

'Get out, Emily.'

'No!' she yelled defiantly. There were no alternatives but she felt it important not to capitulate. She began to shiver convulsively as the chill seemed to enter her bones.

Luke cursed, then she watched, horrified, as he waded into the water. She emitted a strangled squeak as he scooped her up in his arms and carried her out of the loch. After one startled, scared glance into his blue eyes, she shut her own tightly. His were too observant and she was incapable of disguising the impact the damp contact was having upon her. She was held captive, not just by his arms but by the erotic sensations that were scalding her. Sweat mingled with the salt water, making her skin slick beneath her waterlogged nightdress. She felt intoxicated, defenceless under the weight of desire the touch of him evoked.

He remained silent when she linked her hands around his neck, although she heard his sharp inhalation and felt his chest rise and fall rapidly. She allowed her head to fall against the breadth of his chest, knowing she would probably regret this weakness later. The security was an illusion, but it was blissful. She drank in the musky male scent of him, took note of every minute detail of him, knowing she'd replay the sensations later on...

He placed her on the kitchen floor and she felt something inside her protest as the intimate contact was broken. A small pool of water was developing around her feet, and she contemplated the sight with deep interest.

'Fairly stupid even by your standards.' The deep timbre of his voice was strained. She raised her eyes reluctantly. He looked like some dark, austere angel, her fallen Lucifer, emanating disapproval. He raked his dark hair with his fingers. He was wet up to mid-thigh, the material of his jeans clinging to the outline of his legs. A deep carnation stained the rounded contour of her smooth cheeks and she looked away. 'The water is several metres deeper a little further along.'

'I can swim,' she said in an offhand manner which through her eyelashes she could see irritated him enormously. The fact satisfied a perverse desire to aggravate him.

'You're freezing,' he observed, watching the faint tremors she couldn't suppress. 'You need to get out of that thing.' His eyes were burning ferociously in the tense stillness of his face. The nightdress, wet, made her appear almost more naked than no clothes at all. It clung to the upthrust of her full breasts and followed the dip and flare of her waist and hips, as did his eyes.

Emily didn't move; she couldn't. She waited, breath suspended, her whole body in tune with the wild fire that sang through her veins. She didn't want to run, escape; she wanted... He took a step towards her, his eyes never leaving her face.

Emily almost spoke the words—a plea fighting to escape was on her tongue. He bent forward, picked up a blanket that lay on the sofa and flung it at her. Automatically she caught it.

'Get dry.' He slung a rucksack across his shoulder and with a terse, 'I'll be back before dark,' was gone.

Her, 'I hate you!' was shouted at a half-open door. Clutching the blanket, she sank down cross-legged on to the floor and let the sobs emerge.

She had to stop eventually, but when she did she found there had been nothing cathartic about the outburst; she still felt as wretched as ever. He had walked out just like that— after building up her desire to fever pitch, he could walk away. She'd been about to forget all her pride. It was like a form of insanity, this yearning; it was so powerful, so deaf and blind to the mundane precepts of self-preservation.

She stripped off her wet clothes slowly, lethargically, and tried to rub some life back into her limbs along with some circulation. Luke had gone out half saturated and half dressed himself. She quashed a brief, sharp spasm of concern, a concern that would have afforded him considerable amusement, she was sure. She felt wilted with a deep sense of anticlimax. She should be grateful for his sudden exit. Had he known she was on the brink of surrender? Is that all he wants? she wondered. To break me down? Was that the aim of his verbal assault, this refined torture? He's not actually interested in the end result; he just needs to make me admit my fatal weakness, all the lies. Then she recalled a lick of the compelling hunger in his eyes she'd been immobilised by, and the theory crumbled.

CHAPTER SEVEN

IT HAD BEEN the most miserable day in her memory. She had had to cope with another telephone conversation with her father, who had managed to get the telephone number, which was, she was sure, unlisted. Like Luke, he too could be persistent to the point of obsession, which was one reason why the hostilities between them would go on indefinitely, she realised.

She had fielded his questions carefully, coped with his alternate pleading and abuse. When he'd demanded whether she was aware that Luke was just using her, she'd almost wept; but it hadn't been that which had thrown her, it had been the one question, 'Do you love him?' It had hit her like a bolt of lightning. She'd heard her father's indrawn breath as she'd replied, unable at that point to dissimulate. 'Tell him I'll flay him if he hurts you,' had been the only response he had made before he'd hung up.

She hadn't mentioned the phone call to Luke, but then even when he had finally returned they had communicated mainly with cold glances. He had treated her as though she were part of the furniture, and finally she had retreated to her small bedroom before it was even dark. The paperback she'd taken from a bookshelf would normally have made her oblivious to her surroundings for hours; but tonight she hadn't been able to concentrate, though she had memorised the first page word for word—well, she had read it countless times.

She saw the light under the door indicate that Luke had

retired too and saw it extinguished. Sleep was elusive even in the small hours, and the hand she'd scalded the previous night was still throbbing. It was a superficial burn, red and raw but none the less painful. She recalled seeing a medicine box in the dresser and in desperation decided to try and find some pain-killers to dull the throb.

Creeping through Luke's room was traumatic, but she tried to ignore the large bulk outlined in the bed. Downstairs, she went directly to the dresser and discovered to her relief that there was a bottle of pain-killers.

'What exactly are you doing?'

She leapt and the bottle clattered to the floor, spilling the contents over the stone flags. 'Now see what you've made me do,' she accused, close to tears.

Luke retrieved the bottle and looked thoughtfully at her. 'What do you need these for?' His eyes caught the furtive movement as she tucked her injured hand behind her back. 'The coffee last night?' He caught the wrist she tried to conceal, an expression of fury on his face. 'Hiding it won't make it go away. You've been in pain all this time?'

'It's nothing.'

'Superficial,' he agreed, eyes raised to brush her face, taking in the signs of strain and blue bruised discolouration beneath her wide-spaced eyes. 'Hurts like hell, though.' He continued to examine the inflamed area.

Emily swallowed. She'd been ready to scream at his initial cool diagnosis, but the sympathetic addition made her throat ache with a sudden rush of tears. Tenderness from Luke, even as impersonal as this, delivered a mortal blow to her new vulnerability.

'A bit,' she admitted in a breathy whisper.

'It could have been avoided.'

The blue eyes were intent, the spurt of irritated anger having given way to unfamiliar concern. Emily felt her body clench as she fought to tear her eyes away from his dark face. 'You're still dressed.' She had only just realised he was still wearing a pale denim shirt and darker blue jeans.

'I wasn't anticipating sleep.' The curve of his mouth was sensual, the rasp in his voice ironic. His voice was filled with a puzzling self-mockery. Emily realised just how close to exhaustion he looked.

Her uninjured hand went out as if to touch his chest, the impulse too strong to counter. She looked at her own hand as if surprised to see it there, a hair's breadth from his solid, warm reality. With a sharp inhalation she snatched it back as though it too were burnt.

Luke's stillness was almost frightening; there was a tension emanating from him that for a split-second she was positive would explode into action. He was breathing slowly, the inhalations laboured, as if he was consciously controlling the process.

'Sit there.' The curt command was so ridiculously rational compared to what her imagination had been anticipating that she felt sure all the unspoken sexual tension had been born of her rampant frustration. Hot with a sudden painful humiliation, she subsided into a chair. Her arm throbbed and her head ached with a bleak, penetrating misery.

'Keep your arm in that. I've got some bandages in the car.'

She shuddered as the cold water came into contact with her hot flesh, but it did dull the throb of insistent pain. Luke left the door open as he disappeared and the intense night fragrance drifted into the room almost like a physical presence. She inhaled and relaxed slightly, letting a warm, diffuse drowsiness temporarily snuff her anxieties.

She raised her head sleepily from the crook of her arm on the table-top when he entered carrying a box. Silently she watched him competently extract several items.

'Have you taken any pain-killers yet?'

'I don't need...' His presence somehow made other more

painful sensations take supremacy over the superficial injury... Some wounds went deeper.

'Preserve me from martyrs and swallow these,' he said in a tone that indicated he felt inclined to push them down her throat if she offered further resistance. 'Now, let's have a look at the damage.' He bent close, intent on examining the extent of the scald which, although she knew it was minor, was extremely painful. 'It's blistered.' His touch was gentle, if clinical, but his voice held a raw anger. 'If you'd had the sense to immerse it under cold water at the time none of this would be necessary,' he chastised, taking a dry dressing from its bag. 'I'll put a dressing on; it'll be more comfortable that way. What the hell were you thinking of?'

'I did,' she protested, but he ignored her. She watched the deft way he wound a crêpe bandage around her arm. What would he say, she wondered, if she told him exactly what she had been thinking of? White bandage and brown fingers transposed until her vision became a blur; the silence grew shrill and insistent in her ears.

'Luke...'

The sensation of being carried by a pair of male arms close against a hard torso had an addictive quality. Hazily she knew she ought to open her eyes, but it seemed a shame to break into this delightful interlude.

'Emily, are you awake?'

The irate tone dispelled the nice fantasy of being cradled in a lover-like embrace. 'I think so,' she admitted guiltily.

'It speaks! Then for God's sake open the bloody door.'

She snapped her eyes open. 'There is no need to swear,' she croaked.

'If I drop you on the floor I can open it myself.'

'I find that scenario preferable.'

And he did; he actually did! She sat in stunned disbelief on the bare polished boards of the hallway. 'How dare you?' She picked herself up and strode into the room.

'You're a barbarian!' she yelled after him. Then she froze. 'What are you doing?' Her voice came after a breathless interval. She couldn't tear her eyes away; he seemed to her the essence of sensuality. She turned her head away as he unbuckled the leather belt around his waist, but she could still hear the rustle as he removed his jeans.

She felt frantic to escape the room—just looking at him made the nerve-endings pulse with painful life beneath her skin. The dragging sensation was truly magnetic; it made her feel as if she was being pulled in disparate directions.

'I'll leave you to it, then.'

'To what, exactly? Another sleepless night?' he enquired with heavy irony. 'To wonder what stunt you'll come up with next? Maybe drive into the nearest loch?' he suggested. 'I wouldn't put any stupidity past you. I mean, if I hadn't been here, what exactly would you have done about the scald, and who would have stopped you smashing your skull on the stone flags? You literally jumped into the loch. I've seen kittens with more sense of self-preservation,' he stormed.

'I don't faint!' she insisted, ignoring the evidence to the contrary. 'Besides, if it weren't for you I wouldn't be here *to* scald myself or faint. And I *fell,* I didn't jump,' she reminded him. 'I have no suicidal tendencies.' She gave a gasp of instant regret and took an impetuous step towards him. 'Luke, that was...' His expression didn't encourage her to go further. 'I'm catching this bloody disease,' she said, furious and ashamed of the malicious retort that had sprung to her lips. 'I won't waste all my energies on spite,' she told him soberly. 'You're dominated by it, it motivates everything you do, even taking me to bed. It's twisting you. Tell me, what's your incentive for getting up each morning if it's not to plan the next move in your grand scheme?'

'Tomorrow is already planned,' he said, his voice cold and passionless. 'We go to London, at which point we can announce to our families—or should I say family—the news of our impending nuptials.'

She shuddered, feeling despair—not that she'd expected anything she said to alter the course of events; she was a minor player...cannon fodder. 'I don't think Dad will be exactly surprised. He rang today.'

'You told him?' His incredulity was obvious.

She gave a small, grim smile. 'I wouldn't deprive you of that pleasure,' she said bitterly. 'Let's just say I implied...things.' She gave a helpless shrug; she could hardly tell him what she had said. 'Would you really tell him the lies about me—us?' she asked tremulously.

'It would be the ultimate humiliation, wouldn't it?' he mused. 'To imagine I had seduced his baby girl and discarded her...while he was in the house. I think that would be a nice touch. I could have, Emily, couldn't I?' he tormented her coldly. 'It's a tough decision but on the whole I think an entrée to the charmed inner circle and smiling acceptance through clenched teeth might be even more amusing. "My son-in-law"... I can hardly wait.'

Seething, burning hatred was easier to contemplate than this calculating war of attrition she was forced to participate in. 'The marriage will be a mockery,' she protested huskily. It was all so sordid, so ugly; but she still loved him despite all logic and she suspected she always would.

'And what would your marriage to Gavin have been?' he demanded tautly. 'This marriage will give us both things we need.'

She gave a scornful laugh. 'Sex, you mean,' she said disparagingly.

'You certainly respond to me on that level, and it does seem to be preying on your mind, infant,' he said softly. 'As a rule women do respond to me on other levels.'

'I hate you and I wish you'd stayed away!' she spat at him. 'Four years—I thought you'd never come back.'

'Is that why you were marrying Gavin?'

'Dream on,' she sneered. It was a part of the truth, she realised with horror. How long had she been subconsciously holding herself back from involvement, waiting?

'You say sex as though it's sordid, unclean; I think, with us, sex could be quite beautiful,' he said throatily, his eyes fixed hungrily on her frozen countenance. 'What are you afraid of, Emmy?'

'I'm a Stapely,' she reminded him hoarsely. His voice, his delicious rough velvet drawl, was teasing the aching hunger into full flowering life.

'I don't need reminding,' he said jerkily as she licked her dry lips with the tip of her tongue. The atmosphere in the room was electric.

'Why are you crying? Is it your arm hurting?' he asked. The concern was masked by a rough, impatient tone, but she could hear it lapping the edges of his voice. He took a step towards her and his thumb stroked the downward path of a tear.

'No, the pain-killers are working,' she said swiftly, silently cursing her inability to lie conveniently. The next obvious question could have been avoided. She awaited the inevitable, her mind already searching for a reasonable reply.

'Why the tears?' A finger this time traced the downward course of a single salty droplet. She let out a cry of protest, which he ignored. She instinctively lifted her arms to cover her face, afraid of the emotion spilling out of her.

'Turn it out,' she pleaded huskily, indicating the lamp. She was still quivering from the simple impersonal contact of one finger tip. God only knew what he'd see in her face, her eyes.

'I don't want you to hide in the darkness, Emmy, not from me, not tonight.'

Something in his voice, the sensuous yearning, the raw unrefined quality, made her tightly shut eyes flicker open. His face, the taut, rigid lines, the burning, almost feverish glow in his azure gaze toppled her off the precarious emotional tightrope she'd been walking these past two days. She didn't have the mental reserves or the desire to fight the prowling hunger that stalked her waking and sleeping moments. Right now, Luke wanted her; and she had to accept that that was all he had to offer.

Perhaps the pain is part of it, she thought, reaching out with a trembling hand to touch his jaw, rough with a dark shadow that grated across her fingertips. 'Luke?' She felt the violent shudder that ran through his body.

'Do you know what you're doing to me, woman?' he asked, none of the skilled negotiator of obstacles in his voice now; it was raw, needy.

It was the need that pushed her past her limit of endurance. She made a soft sound in her throat and walked into his open arms. They closed around her like steel bands, and together they fell on to the tumbled bedclothes.

'Please, Luke, I want you,' she gasped, feeling transformed by her sudden surrender to the torrent of emotional and physical cravings. He was supporting his upper body weight over her, close but not touching. She felt that she should say something more articulate about her need, her surrender to that need, but her throat closed over raw emotion. She felt a sudden surge of panic at his lack of response; she'd mistaken the moment. Mortification made her grow cold. Only the sudden weight of Luke's body stopped her turning sinuously away. She began to struggle regardless.

'Stop it, you little fool.' His voice was close to her ear, she could feel the warmth of his breath on her neck, hear the harsh tone of his breath. His hands bunched in her hair, immobilising her head, forcing her to look into his face. 'What the hell do you think I'm going to do?' he demanded savagely.

'I made a mistake.' She couldn't. He was using her. Being held so close, so intimately that she couldn't begin to...

His mouth on her face, neck, the upper slope of her breasts was a breathless, compelling seduction of her senses. She felt weak, compliant, aching with the need for fulfilment.

'Luke…?' His eyes never left her face as he removed the single garment she wore. The blaze of raw, unvarnished passion in his eyes was a revelation.

'I want to watch you while I make love to you,' he murmured huskily, one hand running the length of her from the delicate curve of her collarbone to the quivering smoothness of her thigh, where it came to rest possessively. The sight of his hand against her own flesh was indescribably erotic. She wondered how every slight movement could be so arousing, so exciting. A slow-burning fuse had exploded in her brain into incandescence.

He caressed her body with an agonising patience, precision, as if memorising each feminine dip and curve. He contemplated the full mounds of pink-tipped flesh, feasting himself on the feel and taste of her, following the blue-veined tracery and the swollen ruched peaks until she cried hoarsely in protest.

In the thick, voluptuous silence their eyes met. He was panting as hard as she was as she slowly and deliberately allowed her fingers to glide provocatively over sweat-slicked skin. Tentatively almost, she slid lower across his flat belly, letting her lips and tongue revel in the taste and scent of him. The raw, elemental sound that was ripped from his throat touched something primitive within her, and her nails bit into his flesh as her teeth grazed the flatness of his nipple.

'I want to watch you too,' she said suddenly.

Luke's laugh was a fierce, heady mixture of male satisfaction, triumph and tenderness. He rolled over and she welcomed the enveloping weight of his hard body. 'Shall I tell you what I intend to do to you, Emmy?' he murmured throatily, his teeth against her ear sending a series of sharp shivers through her. She looked at him with smoky golden eyes, which felt weighted by her eyelashes, and he took this as an affirmative.

The words should have shocked her virginal ears but she felt a wild, uncontrolled excitement as she listened to his warm, deep voice. The mutual caresses and kisses grew less measured, more frantic, as passions escalated like a violent, unstoppable chain reaction.

'Emmy, I can't take much more of this,' he rasped, his breath searingly hot against her neck. Gently but possessively the heel of his palm ground rhythmically into the soft mound of her pubic bone wherein centred the core of her agony.

'Just take me, then,' she pleaded. Did he hesitate? She almost screamed in frustration, then she saw the expression burning in his eyes and her body instinctively opened itself for him.

The intrusion of him was swift and fierce, but tempered. For a split-second her muscles tensed in protest at the sharp pain. 'Don't,' she cried out, wrapping her legs around him to prevent the swift withdrawal she sensed was imminent. 'I want this,' she said with a primitive ferocity, for an instant reversing the aggressive role. Then, as she gave herself up to the rhythm and let it flow through her, there were no roles—just a harmony of giving and taking. She wanted to sob with the enormity of the emotion that filled her, just as he filled her physically.

Just as she thought she'd die from the sheer pleasure of reaching for something tantalisingly out of reach, the demands of Luke's body altered subtly. She welcomed the new elemental, awesome power of him.

He was repeating her name, a hoarse mantra, in her ear. She sobbed out loud as the first deep contraction of pleasure shook her with a shocking ferocity. The cry ripped from Luke's throat mingled with her own voice until they lay inextricably linked in the afterglow of their lovemaking.

WHEN EMILY AWOKE the room was filled with a dusty sunlight that filtered through the curtains, illuminating the room. Memory returned in a sudden rush, not gently, gradually, and she turned to find a pair of blue eyes watching her as recall suspended the present. What was she supposed to say? How casual was she supposed to be? Deep inside, her instincts made her want to express the totality of the love that filled her, spilled out of her. It was there for a split-second before she carefully extinguished all outward expressions of incautious emotion.

For her, last night had been unique, a physical outlet of the love she felt for this man; but he didn't want what she had to offer. For him, it had been a casual if tempestuous encounter; there had been no twin in him of the well in her own breast that had been tapped in the dark hours, opening her mind and body to the ecstasy of fulfilling the destiny of her womanhood. She couldn't bear the humiliation of him knowing—seeing his scorn, watching the calculation as he assimilated this fresh ammunition in his quest to punish her father.

She had made the biggest mistake in her life, and yet she knew that if she found herself in the same place with the same man she'd not alter a thing. She didn't want to look at him, see triumph on his chiselled, sternly beautiful features. Would he lose any time in taking advantage of the situation he had created? She was a Stapely, the breed responsible for the death of his mother, the same family who had tried to subjugate his anarchic self-sufficiency. He had turned the tables on one of them.

There had to have been more to it than that. Rebellion spilled from some deep inner core. But she ruthlessly quelled the small voice of optimism. She couldn't allow herself to be bewitched by his skill as a lover, to endow it with anything deeper than it had been. To her, it had been an incredible revelation; she'd discovered depths within herself that she'd never dreamt were there to be awoken.

She'd lost the arrogance that had made her assume she could ignore the basic female instincts, but she also knew that only one man would ever awake them—sublimation with some pale imitation would never now be possible.

'What time is it?' You couldn't get much more pragmatic than that, she thought wryly. Disobedient to her control, a portion of her mind was sketching the way her body could fit so perfectly with Luke's long-limbed, hardly muscled frame. The image was intensely satisfying, warm and complacent.

'Emily, throw off the shackles of civilisation just for a few moments. Does it actually matter what time it is?' he asked her, his voice dry. As he raised himself on one elbow the blanket slid down to his waist, and she felt her face colour.

The cool, sophisticated image didn't go with adolescent blushes. 'We can't stay in bed all day,' she muttered, sheltering behind her lowered eyelashes.

'Why not?'

She shot him a startled glance. 'People don't.' The blue eyes looked as guileless as a summer sky, and she felt deeply uneasy. 'I only asked the time,' she grumbled, plucking at the sheet. 'A perfectly normal enquiry. Why you have to dissect every syllable I utter is beyond me.'

Luke rolled over on to his back, but his eyes remained on her face. 'Natural perversity?'

'You have your share of that.'

'I take it we are to avoid any reference to last night.' The guilelessness was replaced by a certain hard implacability.

'My hand is feeling fine, thank you.'

Luke whistled silently through his teeth. 'Emily…' There was a warning in his voice.

'I didn't want to make too much of an isolated incident,' she said cautiously.

'One-night stands being a common occurrence for you,

I take it,' he said in the tone of someone with a deep, if academic interest.

'I wouldn't say that.' Idiot, she told herself miserably; he *did* notice!

'I've never actually slept with a virgin before, but I can still recognise the fact.' He rolled over, one arm thrown over her supine body, the other framing her face, his fingers pushed into the tumbled mass of her hair on the pillow.

Was she supposed to apologise? she wondered, feeling her stomach muscles tighten with the misery of rejection. 'Sorry I didn't match up to your standards,' she said from between clenched teeth. How dared he be angry? Hadn't she given him a gift? While it wasn't one he required, he didn't have to be so brutal about the fact.

'Do you misinterpret everything I say deliberately, or is it a genetic flaw?' he exploded with exasperation. 'You are twenty, you were engaged, for God's sake; I assumed you—'

'Were reasonably competent,' she interrupted bitterly.

Luke swore. 'I could have hurt you.' An expression she thought might have been regret flitted across his face as his quiet statement stilled her. 'There could have been better introductions, less savage, more controlled.'

She blinked, totally confused. 'The experience hasn't scarred me emotionally or physically,' she said gruffly, 'so you must have done something right.'

He looked at her, a glimmer of humour sliding into his eyes. 'How kind of you to say so.'

'I don't think—' she began as he threw one leg over her own, effectively pinning her beneath him. The texture of his hair-roughened skin was abrasive against her softer flesh, and the satisfactory, if elusive male scent of him made the words which were meant to bring distance atrophy in her throat.

'A man has to be flattered to be the first, to sample the sweetness a woman can offer; but why did you wait? Why me, Emmy?' His voice deep and sensual, like the curve of his mouth as he brushed her lips softly.

She'd been waiting for Luke even if she hadn't known it; some destiny had been pushing her in this unlikely direction. A contemplative smile played across her lips as her eyes flickered down the strong column of his throat to the deep muscles of his shoulders, and lower, over the lean, spare, elegant lines of him.

What am I doing? A deep spasm of fear and horror tensed each languor-filled muscle in her body. She was acting as if what she felt was a reciprocal thing, not a secret to be jealously guarded. She could be bemused by a few soft, suggestive words and a kiss, she realised in disgust, knowing how close she'd been to acting like a total fool.

'I admit to a certain curiosity,' she said, her voice cool, her lashes strategically lowered over her eyes—eyes filled with pain. 'I can't say I ever took a vow of celibacy deliberately; circumstances just conspired to make it that way. Gavin respected my wishes not to anticipate the marriage vows, though I now see there was a certain degree of hypocrisy involved in that assurance,' she added drily, not actually feeling touched by her ex-fiancé's infidelity any longer. 'I decided my inexperience would be an obstacle rather than an attribute if I ever intended to have another relationship. And having seen your rather hysterical reaction I'd say I was correct.' She gave a small laugh, her throat dry. 'To be honest, this has been the ideal opportunity. I mean, it's not as if there can be any misunderstandings between us—we don't have to pretend for convention's sake that something deep and meaningful happened beyond the obvious.' She subsided, breathless, awaiting his response.

'I don't recall you being so pragmatic and cool last night,' he hit back. One supple motion brought her on to her side until they lay thigh to thigh, breast to breast. His face was filled with a black fury which she attributed miserably to wounded ego. She'd only said it before he had a chance to, hadn't she? Or was that what he didn't like?

'That, Luke, was then. Same place, different time.' she responded coolly. 'I'd be grateful if you'd let me go; I want a bath.' He was stroking her flank with long, sweeping movements and it was hard to sound unaffected when her insides were dissolving into a golden mist of desire.

'All in good time. I'll fill the bath and even soap your back.' One hand threw back the covers and his eyes strolled unapologetically over her pale body. 'And possibly other parts,' he purred.

She closed her eyes. 'This is ridiculous, Luke. You can't propose to rape me.' She opened her eyes; his were cynical and gleaming. He never would need to. He might have said it, but he didn't need to; it was in the triumphant gleam in his eyes and the feverish desperation in her own. The moment of empathy passed and she was aware of the anger in him. 'I don't want...' she began. 'Not while you're angry.'

'Angry at being told I'm a convenient body?'

'Isn't that what women are to you?' she hit back.

'Just because you are as incapable as the rest of your clan of sustaining a relationship, don't assume I am similarly handicapped. The women I sleep with happen to have been fully rounded—and I don't just mean physically,' he snarled, his derision biting. 'Intellectually and emotionally stimulating is what I'm talking about. Not lifetime partners, but not one-night stands either.'

'Why me, then, if I'm neither, and emotionally retarded into the bargain?' she demanded, her struggles to free herself only succeeding in trapping her arms against his chest. She glared at him defiantly, her breath coming in short, laboured gasps. 'And, most importantly, I'm a Stapely.' And this was his revenge for a lifetime of slights...and one unforgiveable sin.

The laugh was a fragmented sound, seeming to be torn from somewhere deep in his chest. 'Believe it or not, that fact isn't uppermost in my mind at this instant; and I've been asking *myself* why you, why Emily with the eyes that can be seductive and innocent, innocent eyes and erotic mouth… You taste so sweet,' he said with bitterness, his voice thick. She scarcely noticed, her senses were so choked with the aching awareness of him. His mouth was impossible to evade even had she felt the desire any longer to do so. His tongue moved in sensual pantomime of the movement of his hips against her belly. She moaned in his mouth, growing limp and pliant, surrendering with some relief to the inevitability.

'I want to hear you say it.' His voice was slurred, his eyes glittering with the sexual fever that held him in its relentless grip. Her head thrashed on the pillow as his voice, as exacting as his body, continued in her ear. 'I waited a long time, Emily; I want to hear you tell me again.'

She felt boneless with supplication. 'I want you, Luke.' Did he need complete capitulation? She wondered bleakly, hearing her own voice respond to his demands just as her body shifted to accommodate his every unspoken desire. 'I want to feel your hands on me…taste you,' she murmured, the words emerging from between a series of small guttural moans.

Her determination never to let this happen again was forgotten as he touched not just her body but an invisible part of herself too long ignored; now it craved the warmth, the passion that he gave her. His hand had been touching the silken flesh of her inner thigh with feather-like, sensitive motions that made her delirious with anticipation, but he had been still too long.

A question in her feverish eyes, she looked into his face.

'After last night I thought you might be sore,' he said with a bluntness which starkly highlighted the new and frightening intimacy between them. Frightening because the longer it went on, the harder it would be for her when he returned to his world and she was no longer useful.

'Would you care?'

'Still playing unwilling victim, Emmy?'

She shook her head, suddenly ashamed of the hasty riposte. He had been nothing if not generous and sensitive as a lover, erotic and passionate. 'I'm not too sore,' she responded huskily. 'If I said I was, what would you do?' she added curiously. His control would have to be of the iron variety if he could switch off at this point.

'Shall I show you, my curious, sleek little cat?' he asked as he firmly parted her thighs. Emily's reply was all that he could have wished.

CHAPTER EIGHT

SHOULD SHE WEAR the green dress or was it too formal? With a sigh of despair Emily threw it on top of several other discarded outfits on the bed. The bed she had shared with Luke for the past three weeks. His London flat occupied the entire floor of a converted warehouse; it was elegantly uncluttered, with a gleaming wooden floor scattered with vibrant oriental rugs and a tasteful mixture of antique and modern furniture. It was remarkably well-organised, if you discounted the books which overflowed on to most available surfaces.

'Shouldn't you have a shower?'

She didn't turn at the sound of his voice. 'Is that your way of telling me I smell?' she said calmly, although as always her metabolic rate kicked into a higher gear because of his presence.

'You smell of me,' he said, coming behind her and taking the weight of her breasts in his hands, his thumbs touching the sensitised nubs through her thin robe. She turned her head to meet his contemplative stare.

She didn't need any reminder to recall the afternoon they'd spent. She shivered as the erotic, sensuous pictures played in her head, and her hands came up to grip his forearms which encircled her. A slow smile curved her lips as her eyes fell on the tumbled bedclothes. He bent his head and his mouth moved over her nape.

The weeks they had been together had made her aware of a sensual side of her nature that was both shocking and

delightful. She greedily relished her role as eager pupil—
all she had withheld was the verbal confirmation of her
love. The restraint was painful but necessary. Whatever
happened in the future, she had her memories, and she
hugged them to herself, determined not to be robbed.

'Are you nervous?' he asked.

'What do you care?' she flung at him. He didn't try to
stop her pulling away. She stared at him with dark-eyed
resentment; his words had spoilt the sweetness of the moment.

'You have to see them some time.'

'Of course I do; that's what I'm here for, isn't it?' she
accused bitterly. As if she needed reminding. 'At least it's
on neutral territory. I should be glad, in the circumstances,
for any small mercy. I don't suppose even you and Dad
can brawl in public.' Tonight was the first time she had
seen her family since Luke had informed them of the engagement. No matter what went on in private, the recrim-
inations and bitterness, in public at least the Stapelys would
simulate acceptance of the situation.

'I've not noticed you complaining,' he observed, his sensuous mouth betraying the cruelty she knew he was capable
of.

'Perhaps I'm making the best of what is, after all, a temporary arrangement,' she responded coolly. 'Someone like
you is all right for short-term passion, but you're hardly
equipped for anything more intense. Not with your gypsy
blood.' Her teeth gouged a groove in her full lower lip to
stop it trembling.

'You mean my uncertain parentage,' he said, his voice
hardening. 'I've always enjoyed the latitude that allowed
me. I didn't have to be saddled with a pompous, pretentious, narrow-minded, avaricious bastard.' He shot her a
look of dark dislike. 'What is it with you? You seem more
comfortable when we're flinging insults at one another.'

She took a deep breath. She hadn't meant anything of

the sort, but his casual vitriol was sincere. 'I've heard you described in equally glowing terms,' she said drily. 'And it's what we do best, isn't it, fling insults?'

'I wouldn't say that,' he said throatily. The smoky purr made her knees grow weak. 'Did you defend my honour?' he wondered drily.

'Why should I?' she retorted, holding on to the dressing-table to steady herself. 'They are my family; you're…'

'The poor relation to be displayed on suitable occasions to illustrate the open-hearted generosity of the glorious Stapelys.'

'You always seemed well able to take care of yourself,' she muttered mutinously. Had she fared so much better? She had a brother with whom she had nothing in common, a sister who stole her fiancé—as it happened a favour—and parents who had never hidden the fact that she was a major disappointment. Parents to whom her wishes, her desires had never been anything other than an inconvenience. 'Families aren't all they are cracked up to be. Maybe I envied you. I think you're just twisted by self-pity; the great laid-back Lucas Hunt is consumed by mean, petty self-interest.'

The leap of emotional response in his eyes made a *frisson* of unease crawl the length of her spine. 'Maybe you *are* the loser,' he agreed surprisingly. 'I doubt if you were ever on the receiving end of any genuine emotion. I had my mother for at least part of my childhood and, although by your standards we were poor, at least I learnt how to give and receive affection.' He gave a shrug, his lip curling. 'You, on the other hand, never had the lessons, and they do say if you've never had love you're never able to function fully. I mean, it gives pause for thought when a woman is still a virgin at twenty.'

'Was!' she yelled, incredibly wounded by the denouncement of her character. It was her ability to love that was inflicting such torment at that precise moment.

'I stand corrected,' he drawled.

'I'd hardly equate an afternoon of sex with you as an emotional high,' she yelled.

'Is that a fact?' he said with narrow-eyed interest. 'What exactly would you call it?' he enquired silkily.

'A technical learning experience,' she shot back.

He dived for her, his features a dark, angry blue. 'You really can be a prize little bitch.'

'Blame the genetic pool,' she said with flippancy born of a sense of extreme loss. 'It seems to be a fixation of yours.' She twisted to free herself from his grasp. Luke despised her so much that every time she began to think they could at least be friends his prejudices swirled to the surface like oil on a pool.

'I blame you, you vindictive little wretch,' he snarled. 'Why am I letting you do this to me?' The words were wrenched from him. She could hardly believe the throb of uncharacteristic frustration. It made her stare at him in wide-eyed confusion. What was she doing to him? What did he mean? She saw no answer in his face, only anger that before her eyes transformed into sensual desire. 'You're a sensual little witch.' He made the throaty observation an accusation.

She shivered in swift surrender as he pulled her roughly against him, and accepted the deep, bruising kiss that was both urgent and angry. When her eyes, heavy-lidded, flickered open he was watching her with raw, hot passion glittering feverishly in his blue eyes.

'Technically, how did that rate?' he enquired, his voice slightly slurred and the sharp angle of his high cheekbones highlighted by a faint flush. He smiled with grim satisfaction as she gave a small moan in reply to his hand reaching beneath her shirt to locate unerringly the sensitised peak of one full breast. 'On a scale of one to ten, that is,' he continued casually, not pausing in his delicate exploration of her yielding body.

'Ask me again when I've more room for comparison,' she spat back, outrage at his callous ability to arouse her mingling with a compelling swell of sensuality.

His eyes narrowed to slits. 'Curtail this urge to experiment until I've finished with you,' he advised grimly.

It wasn't the arrogance of his words that made her grow still, it was the reminder of how impermanent his need for her was. He had virtually said he had every intention of discarding her; the marriage licence carrying tomorrow's date would only be legally bonding until the divorce. I already knew that, she reminded herself. Don't let it hurt…don't let him see.

'I think you'll find, Luke, I have something to say on the matter.' She'd escape before he tired of her, she swore silently to herself.

'What do you have to say then, Emmy?' he enquired with open contempt. Arms around her waist, he bodily hoisted her upwards until their hips were level, leaning forward until her back was against the wall.

Her head fell backwards as his teeth drew blood from the tender flesh of her lips. The feeling of surrender was washing over her in great tidal waves. In this position it was impossible to ignore the arousal of his body, and the slight friction between them was enough to make her feel weak with desire. Speak? She didn't feel she could breathe! Her lungs felt depleted of oxygen and her head was spinning. Did he have to illustrate so cruelly just how easily he could make her retract her impulsive words…how in charge he was while she was being whisked along, a victim of blind, relentless passion?

'Luke, the door,' Emily gasped as her brain registered the repeated, the strident peal.

'To hell with them,' he said huskily.

'I need to get dressed,' she reminded him, pulling away and catching the lapels of her robe together. The blue eyes, dark with smouldering passion, snapped with frustration.

'Wear the blue,' he threw over his shoulder as he padded barefoot into the open-plan living area. She instantly chose the green.

'My dear Luke, it's very naughty of you not to let me know you were here.' The silence combined with the voice made Emily tighten the sash around her waist and stalk into the living-room.

She paused, her mouth agape, to see an elegant blonde. Her long hair was sleekly drawn back to reveal a swan-like neck, and she had her arms around Luke. The clothes proclaimed their owner's financial and social status very clearly—a designer combination of classical tailoring and innovative, jewel-bright fabrics.

Emily made an inarticulate sound in her throat; rage swept through her like a tidal wave and the two came up for air.

'Won't you introduce us, Luke?' Blue eyes coldly skimmed Emily's dishevelled figure. 'I have to discover by accident—' the smile touched Luke and widened almost to encompass Emily '—that he is in London. I'm Luke's nearest neighbour in Scotland,' she explained, her fingers playfully running up and down Luke's forearm. 'Once in a while I check his place there hasn't totally collapsed when it's empty, and get major damage like gaping holes in the roof repaired. I thought, darling, we were doomed to pass like ships in the night. But you've been here all along.'

Emily smiled in a strained way. 'Luke must be very grateful,' she murmured drily.

'Luke can be an angel, can't he, if he can be bothered? The rest of the time he's hopeless. Don't you think?' The sly, laughing glance was intercepted by a unruffled Luke. A beautifully manicured hand was stretched out to Emily. 'I'm Beth Urquhart, as Luke has quite forgotten his manners. Call me Beth.'

Emily somewhat self-consciously accepted the pearly-nailed hand. 'I'm Emily *Stapely*.' She found herself emphasising her surname and casting Luke a half-challenging look from beneath the sweep of her lashes. I'm damned if I'm going to apologise to her, you, or anyone else for my name, the look said, and the flicker in his eyes told her the message had been received. She checked for signs of recognition on the other girl's face and detected none.

'Well, Emily, are you staying long with Luke, or is it just an afternoon visit?' The implication of the sordid and trivial nature of their liaison was masterly.

Luke stared passively at Emily's red face. 'Emily is aware of the ultimate privilege. She's living here.'

'A sort of house-sitter. Where are you off to next, Luke?'

The woman was either totally dense or wilfully blind, and obviously besotted with Luke. The insults delivered in the exquisitely modulated tone were making Emily want to scream. What sort of woman accepted that a man she was obviously laying claim to took another woman to bed? 'It's terribly good of you to clean for Luke,' Emily said quietly. 'The cottage was in excellent order.' Two could play that game! With pleasure she saw the older woman stiffen. The steady throb of acid jealousy was making her dizzy.

'I was led to believe he can't bear distractions while he's working in Scotland,' the blonde said, her tone sharp. But when she looked towards Luke there was only blatant adoration. It made Emily feel sick. She felt totally excluded, which had no doubt been the object of the exercise. Beth obviously regarded Luke as her property north of the border. Emily's presence in the cottage had gone down very badly.

'Emily's been helping with the typing.'

'That's me, general girl Friday and all-round good sport,' she agreed with a brisk and good-natured smile. The look she flashed Luke promised reprisal for this categorising as the hired menial. Never do to upset the girlfriend, would it? The bland smile it was received with made her even white teeth grate and her jaw ache with the effort to maintain her own vacuous grin.

'I could have arranged that for you, Luke.'

'But you do so much for me, sweetheart,' Luke drawled. He gave a laconic smile and sent Emily a challenging look. 'I couldn't impose, darling.'

That'll be a first, Emily thought, suppressing the childish interruption that sprang to her lips. The casual endearment was murmured with a smug relish. If they think I'm going to depart tactfully, she thought furiously, reading several chapters between the lines, they can think again. The attraction of the north of Scotland was suddenly a great deal clearer. She cursed herself for a fool for not realising Luke would always have a female at hand wherever he went. 'That's Luke for you—all sweet consideration and old-world charm. The ultimate Boy Scout.'

'Anything you can't handle, Miss Stapely?'

Emily was aware of Luke's narrow-eyed scrutiny as the challenge was issued. 'Call me Emily, please, Beth.' Simpering didn't come easily but she imagined her present expression came as near as she'd ever get. If Luke thinks I'm going to brawl for his favours he can live with disappointment, she thought, feeling no urge to emulate the other woman's blatant tactics. 'Actually, there's the small matter of a wedding tomorrow; if you'd substitute I'd be eternally grateful.' And let 'call me Beth' make of that what she likes, she thought viciously. This tall, elegant woman symbolised every other predictably gorgeous woman she'd ever seen Luke with, and as such didn't inspire warmth and friendliness in her breast. I hope he has one hell of a job smoothing this one over, she asserted silently.

Beth went rigid, the classically perfect face white, her eyes seeking Luke, waiting for him to disprove this claim.

'Wait in the bedroom, Emily.'

Emily had already interpreted the signals the older woman was broadcasting. Fear... She felt a strange empathy. Wasn't this how she felt too? She suddenly felt ashamed of enjoying the pain she'd inflicted. But at Luke's terse command she stiffened.

Silently, head held high, she left them. She stood behind the door, her heart pounding. This was the way it would be. Luke had no intention of altering his lifestyle; he might even bring his women here, as if *she* didn't exist. He had actually dismissed her! The door hadn't closed properly and voices began to make themselves clear above the thunderous roar of her own blood pounding in her ears.

'You're not taking advantage of this child, are you, Luke?'

'I'm marrying Emily, Beth.'

'I understand, Luke. You've been so patient with me.' The throb of emotion made the cultured voice sound less brittle. Emily held her breath, straining to catch each word.

'Patience doesn't enter into it, Beth.'

'I'd never have survived without you after Martin died. I was so angry with him for…daring to leave me.'

'Perfectly natural…'

'It took a long time for me to grieve properly.' Again the throb of emotion, the vulnerability she was allowing Luke to see, made Emily want to cry out in protest.

'You've got to look to the future, Beth, and stop feeling guilty for a normal reaction. You have everything to look forward to.'

'I took off the ring, did you notice?' The woman's voice was breathless, excited.

'I noticed and I'm happy for you, Beth.'

'For us, Luke. Don't you see, we can build a life together? I've buried Martin at last; I can build a new future. I blame myself that you've turned to this child.'

The silence went on for an eloquent eternity. Emily closed the door carefully with a soft click.

By the time Luke returned, Emily already had a small bag packed. She felt cold, composed, and just a little dead.

His eyes swiftly assessed the scene. 'What the hell is going on?'

'I'm leaving.' This is what it feels like to have hope extinguished, she realised, taking a denim jacket and sliding her arms into it. The relentless flame of optimism she'd sustained on the meagre substance at her disposal was just a smoky memory. 'I'm not going to marry you, Luke. I'm sorry if that deprives you of the opportunity to gloat.' She shrugged and went to pick up the small case.

Luke beat her to it. He deliberately emptied the hurriedly packed contents on to the floor and ground his heel into the resulting pile. 'You're not going anywhere.' His expression was remote, icy, the danger of eruptive fury in the inhuman control.

'You can keep those,' she said, ignoring this statement. 'I'll leave in what I stand up in.' All the vitality had drained from her voice, but not her determination. 'Comfort yourself with the knowledge that Dad will crumble when you tell him your lies. It should keep you warm at nights when Beth isn't available. I hope you'll make my apologies to her.'

'Beth has gone,' he said flatly.

'This juggling of women must get tiresome,' she said with narrow-eyed sympathy.

'I don't love Beth, Emmy. Listen…'

'Love!' she snorted. 'I never for a moment imagined you did. I doubt if you're capable, but she loves you.'

'Martin, her husband, was a friend of mine. I was with him when he was killed in Beirut three years ago.'

'Is that why she feels so guilty? I suppose you were having an affair then. Isn't it convenient that now she wants to make it official you're engaged? You like your liaisons to be disposable, don't you, Luke? Am I to be your excuse to keep her at arm's length?'

'You're blindly jealous.' Anger was licking the edges of

control from his voice. 'It doesn't pay to listen to half a conversation,' he said grimly. 'Trust me, Emily.'

She gave a brittle laugh. 'Trust you? That's a contradiction in terms, Luke. Distrust, suspicion and scheming are the activities I instinctively link with your name. I can't stomach it any more. As for jealous,' she jeered spitefully, 'you seem to forget why I'm here to begin with. You hardly think I'd have chosen you as a lover without being blackmailed into it, do you? Your problem is you still think I'm a naïve little schoolgirl, and you had me convinced of the same thing too. I'm calling your bluff, Luke... Anything has to be preferable to marriage to you,' she said fiercely. 'I made a mistake when I slept with you, but I don't intend to compound it by staying here...and—' her voice trembled as she looked at the bed and the evocative evidence of its recent occupation '—repeating the same mistake.' Her eyes remained dry, but her chest heaved with violent emotion.

'If that is the case I don't think there's much more to say, is there?' A light behind his eyes seemed to have been switched off; they were just as blue, but blank...dead. 'You really don't think I'm capable of recognising a moral, let alone displaying principles, do you, Emily?'

Their eyes locked and she shivered convulsively at the icy contempt. 'I think you save your moral crusades for the television screen. Your personal life seems totally devoted to your crusade for revenge.'

'I'm deeply touched by this display of faith,' he drawled, his expression one of refined disgust. 'I have always derived satisfaction when I've managed to disturb the synthetically perfect Stapely household, but do you really think I'm insecure enough to give this priority in my life? Besides, all preconceptions, all parameters can be re-drawn for certain women.' His voice had the texture of raw silk, and she stared at him in fascinated half-comprehension. 'Special women, women capable of giving and trusting— an awesome amount of power to place in the hands of an inconsistent female, but then men too have their vulnerabilities.' The nerve in his right cheek clenched erratically and his eyes burned with zealot-like fervour.

'There's nothing for me here?' It was Beth Urquhart he wanted. He was telling her in the cruellest way possible that she, Emily, had only ever been a minor event, like his attempts to redress the injustice his mother had suffered. Beth was the major attraction, the one that could elicit such stark intensity. She willed him to respond; it was pathetic and she knew it, but at that moment anything from him, any sign of contrition, any tenderness, would have been enough to keep her there. She wanted to belong here with him, exclusively.

His expression remained stony, remote, unyielding. He didn't want her, exclusively or otherwise. If he did, he'd stop her. She walked out of the door, her heart breaking; she could almost hear the sound...

CHAPTER NINE

EMILY SMOOTHED the simple blue silk shift she wore; the antique gold chain around her neck looked faintly sybaritic against the simplicity of the garment, which relied on her slender figure to give it impact. Not for much longer, she thought wryly, surveying the increased curve of her breasts outlined against the fabric. She allowed Gavin to take her jacket and shook her head to free the loose tendrils of hair that softened the elegant chignon where they had caught in the collar.

'You look tremendous.'

Emily accepted the compliment with a warm smile. She was glad they were friends again, and Gavin appeared to have accepted that they would never be anything more. She had literally bumped into him in a department store, but his acceptance of the situation had taken the initial strain from their relationship. She had enjoyed the occasional meal they had had together since she'd moved into her own small flat.

Her best friend Martine had given her the breathing space she'd needed after she'd walked out on Luke. The noise and warmth of the ebullient household with its most recent addition, her six-month-old god-daughter, had made her wistful for all the things she'd missed out on. She had gone through the first few weeks in a numb daze. She didn't want to recall the terrible bleak time, but now she had the incentive to go back out and meet life head-on. She had their child—*her* child, because Luke was not to know. About that she was fiercely determined—the child wouldn't be more ammunition for him. Happiness and fulfilment might be denied her, but they were not prerequisites for a fruitful life; her child was part of Luke that no one could rob her of. When she'd received the confirmation of her pregnancy, one single emotion had risen above the seething mass— joy.

Her first instinct had been to move as far away as possible, but friendly advice had made her realise the benefit of having her friends close at hand; and, while she had no intention of moving back into Charlcot, she didn't want to lose contact with her family completely.

The party was a glittering charity event and she was sure she would bump into other members of her family at some point. It was the sort of high-profile occasion that they felt duty bound to grace with their presence. 'Is Charlotte coming?' she asked innocently, nodding away a drinks tray.

'I wouldn't know.'

She permitted herself a small smile. Despite the recent tiff, she suspected her sister and Gavin would be back together before long. Her eyes skimmed the crowded room, and she was content just to people-watch. The diamonds around necks challenged the glitter of the chandeliers, and she wondered what the starving millions the night was intended to aid would make of it all.

She froze as they traversed the room, and felt the blood drain from her face. Her right hand went out to clutch at Gavin for support. 'I can't stay here...did you know? Hell, I'm going to be sick.'

Her escort's face bore a hunted expression as he glanced around to see if her extraordinary behaviour was drawing unwanted attention. 'Are you ill? Should I get a doctor?'

Seeing the piercing, predatory expression on Luke's face as he got nearer, Emily thought that that might not be such a bad idea. 'Luke...' she muttered in Gavin's ear by way of explanation. What was he doing here? He never attended this sort of party.

The moment she had sensed him, before she'd even seen the tall, distinguished figure impeccable in his evening dress across the room, she had known that her recovery was paper-thin. The awful sense of deprivation that impelled her to say his name out loud sometimes, just to remind herself how it sounded, had been controllable; but this violent rush of emotion was not.

'Hello, Luke.' She felt impelled to be the first to speak, managing to sound at least relatively normal. 'Beth.' She found herself hating the woman with such vehemence that it was almost physical. They would be together; that had been no shock. They looked good—both tall, elegant, she divinely fair and he darkly handsome—a natural pairing. She felt like a shaggy, if cute little Shetland pony beside two thoroughbreds. She felt squashed beneath the oppressive weight of all that perfection.

'Why, this is a real family gathering. I believe Charlie is around here somewhere,' Luke said softly. He'd given Gavin one frankly murderous glare before reserving his attention for Emily. The intense blue of his eyes hit her like a laser. Bland indifference would have been more what she'd expected, and this unbridled aggression threw her even further off balance.

'You and Emily are related?' Beth sounded surprised. If she was put out by the gaping hole in the smooth surface of social behaviour that Luke's unwavering scrutiny had torn, her manner gave no indication. The even white teeth were a great advertisement for advanced dentistry, Emily thought, feeling quite justified in her silent bitchiness.

'We're cousins.'

'I'm by way of being the black sheep in a very respectable clan, Beth. But Emily exaggerates our blood tie considerably. My mother was Charlie Stapely's adoptive cousin; none of the sacred blood runs in my veins.'

'You, a black sheep!' Beth laughed huskily at the

thought. 'I had no idea you were nearly that dangerous, darling. How delicious!'

Emily felt her teeth ache as they clamped together. Did she practise the sultry smile or was it natural flirtatiousness? Either way, she was sure that she herself could never perfect it.

'Luke may not be a Stapely in name, but he has the family trait of feeling secure in his right to use lesser mortals to further his ambitions.' She gave her best unblinking, sweetly simple smile which left enough doubt to make the company unsure of whether she intended to be quite as insulting as she sounded.

The brooding contemplation flared into smouldering anger, and Emily tilted her chin with a defiance she was far from feeling. She tightened her grip on Gavin's arm.

'Our tune, Emily.' She barely had time to blink in shock and rejection before Luke had extricated her from her escort and swung her into the middle of the other couples moving slowly to a nostalgic tune.

'How dare you?' she spat furiously, refusing to look up from his shirt-front. 'We don't have a tune,' she added irrelevantly. It was so hard to think clearly with her body plastered against him, the scent of him awakening sharp memories that made her slither and slide into a sensual morass of endless craving.

The hand in the small of her back performed an intricate arabesque along her spine before pulling her impossibly closer, the lower half of his body making no secret of the effect she was having on him. 'A technical detail, sweetheart. We would have, if you hadn't run out.'

She raised her chin, her eyes glittering in protest. What right had he to sound bitter? 'My memory of the events obviously differs from yours,' she said, too hurt to recall caution. 'I simply didn't care for your ideal of a *ménage à trois,*' she asserted, swirling lights of gold filtering into her wide eyes.

'That's a very provocative little dress,' Luke said, his expression derisory as she made this accusation. 'Does Gavin approve? You really are a creature of habit, aren't you, Emily? Is the wedding back on? You should be an interior decorator for a neat life; you're a natural.'

'You'll be the last to know if it is.' A faint groan escaped her lips as his hand moved over the curve of her behind slowly, sensuously.

'You're generating enough heat to light a small town,' he said, bending his head to rest his chin on the top of hers. She felt the movement of his lips through her hair. 'Does Gavin mind that we were lovers, that I can make you beg for my touch?' The only solid thing at that moment was the seductive whispered words in her ear and the riot of aching, raw sensations. 'Your skin has a special texture, Emmy, satin, transluscent skin. I like to touch you. Can you feel how much I want to touch you?'

She raised her eyes slowly; they felt incredibly heavy, and her heart beat in time to the music's throbbing tempo as their bodies moved in sweet synchronicity to the rhythm. 'Stop it, Luke,' she pleaded hoarsely. She could hear the thunderous thud in his chest, and beneath her fingers the ridge of scar tissue across his ribs stood out. Pleasure at the memory of tracing the old wound with loving lips was mingled with an angry helplessness at the old pain it signified.

He caught her hand and raised it to his lips. With slow deliberation he let the tip of her forefinger move between his lips, tasting. On the surface, the gesture was almost courtly, but he had transformed it into something incredibly erotic. She felt dizzy with the violent response to him and her knees almost buckled as she slumped against him.

'I don't want to stop this… I'm the hedonist, if you recall; self-denial is anathema to me. In a perfect world a man gets what he patiently bides his time for; but this world, infant, is far from perfect.'

'Then it should suit you,' she said, making her voice hard. This self-preservation could be a painful process, she thought miserably. Beth was watching them, she reminded herself, seeking to escape from the voluptuous need for surrender he had evoked with his mastery of her senses.

The deep streak of possessiveness in her nature made her mentally, if not physically, free herself from him. Beth. She was the one Luke really cared for; he had told her as much. He was angry because she had taken the incentive from him and walked out. The profound experience of the communion of their essence was tarnished for her by his perception of the same event. Luke had never lied to her; she knew this. But still the sense of betrayal went deep.

'I'm here with Gavin and you're here with Beth. I see no reason to change that arrangement. Why haven't you told Dad?'

'About what?' he asked, his enigmatic eyes watching her with an unnerving gleam.

'The lies…'

'You have the nerve to talk about lies when you've run back to the tedious safety of pretty boy?'

'Will you stop calling him that?' she bit back. 'He has a name.'

'I doubt if you've been very honest with him, or doesn't he mind being a substitute because you haven't the guts to sustain an adult relationship. If it's a luxurious nest you hanker after, I'm sure I could match anything pretty boy has to offer.'

'The idea of being any man's mistress holds little appeal, but the idea of being yours is absurd. I realise I'm the focus for your ideas of retribution, Luke, but that's absurd. I know Beth's besotted with you, but even she…' A spasm of disgust contorted her face and he relinquished his hold on her as the music stopped, a fact which neither appeared aware of. 'I've only just managed to get my freedom from my father…all of you.'

'Aren't you back at Charlcot?' he said with a frown.

'I have a flat of my own.'

'With Gavin?'

She ignored the thin-lipped query. 'A job, at least a temporary one.' Her legacy from her maternal grandmother would prove very useful in the months to come, when she wouldn't be able to work.

His eyes continued to rake her face. 'There's something else…something different.'

Emily's eyes opened wide with fearful horror. He couldn't put his finger on it now, but he would… Luke almost seemed to be able to see into her skull on occasion.

'You two are making a spectacle for the bored and curious.'

Her father's voice woke Emily from her private world. She flushed, looking around the half-empty floor, aware that they were the target of curious gazes. The expression on Luke's face at being interrupted was so savage that even Charles Stapely lost his edge of suavity and assurance.

'Keep out of this,' Luke ground out. 'I don't know where you get the nerve to warn me to keep away.'

'It was the only way I could ensure you came.'

The music began, leaving the trio a small island of inactivity. These enigmatic words had Luke's complete attention, Emily saw. She could see that once more she was surplus to requirements. She was gone, swallowed up in the well-groomed crowd, before either man had noticed.

EMILY SAT cross-legged on the polished oak floor, the one she had expended so much energy on restoring. Better to fill her time with mindless, exhausting tasks than to be torn by the gut-wrenching longings.

The evening had been a nightmare. She felt numb… Seeing Luke with no prior warning like that had been overwhelming. She had taken a taxi back to her small sanctuary. In a trance-like condition she had thrown off her shoes, undone the clips from her hair, and sunk into her present position. Only the strident peal of the doorbell broke into her abstraction. At first she thought she would ignore it, but it went on and on...

The Smiths, the elderly couple who leased her the top floor of their Victorian villa, were fortunately hard of hearing. The stairs leading to her own private entrance were steep, so she negotiated them with care, ever conscious of the life in her safe-keeping. She was frowning as she wondered how she was going to cope with a pram and this incline as she unbolted the door.

The breath was sucked from her lungs in one great gasping breath. 'Luke!' The possibility of hallucination was discarded. He was totally solid, a tower of savage, simmering rage. How had he found her?

She had sworn Gavin to secrecy.

'You remember my name, then.' He shouldered his way into the narrow hallway and his presence was too overpowering. The greyhound-lean toughness of him was so close she could sense the hard strength of muscles she knew were beneath the formal dress suit he still wore. At some point he'd discarded his tie, and his hair was wildly untidy. She was breathing in air that carried the scent of his body, the unique concoction of odours that produced a natural perfume that made her achingly aware of a deep starvation of her senses.

Her mind was whirling; she refused to look up. Instead she fixed her eyes on the middle button of his pristine shirt. 'I don't know what you're doing here, Luke, but I'd like you to leave,' she said in a surprisingly calm voice. 'We've said all that was necessary.' He'd told her father all those lies, finally gone through with his threat. She'd been waiting for the past ten weeks, wondering why he hadn't, but obviously he'd been waiting for the ideal moment to relish the humiliation. He was here to gloat, punish her with the details.

'Well, what a shame. I don't give a damn what you'd like.'

'Will you lower your voice?' she responded. 'This is a respectable neighbourhood.' He hadn't changed. Still arrogant, overbearing, so bloody sure of himself and to hell with the rest of the world. How did I fall in love with him? she wondered, furious at the elemental response she'd suffered the instant she'd seen him again.

'Then how will they take to having an unmarried mother as a resident?'

Emily looked up, her face swept clear of all colour. 'How… Marty…no, Marty wouldn't,' she stammered in a stunned half-whisper. Martine had promised not to contact Luke even when Emily had confided her condition, and no one else knew yet. The agreement had been grudging, she recalled.

'So glad I have your undivided attention finally,' he drawled. His expression was menacingly aggressive, the blue eyes pure steel. 'Who's Marty, Emmy? Another new boyfriend? Doesn't Gavin come up to scratch?' he asked with a smile that made her swallow down the instinctive scream.

'If you like,' she said defiantly, the air of unconcern spoiled by the spasmodic tremors which swept her entire body.

'It's true, then, you are pregnant?' He watched her, his body coiled like a high-tension spring, the errant nerve in his cheek clenching.

She blinked hard but this nightmare still didn't vanish. A sweetly provoking smile curved itself around her lips. 'Putting truth in the arena would only confuse you, Luke.'

He inhaled sharply, air hissing through his clenched teeth. 'Upstairs.'

'I'm choosy about my guests…' Her words trailed off into a shriek as he literally threw he over his shoulder and carried her fireman style over his shoulder and up the stairs.

He ignored her furious stream of invective and kicked open the half-closed door.

Emily kicked out at him as he placed her on the small sofa, feeling savage satisfaction as her foot connected with his shin. 'You think you can barge in here like some barbarian.' She sat upright, indignation overcoming the instinctive fear the sight of him had produced. Fear that had been well-founded. He knew about the child, though how was a total mystery to her; but that single fact placed in jeopardy her calm, joyful plans. Her newly born maternal instincts were on full alert; if Luke thought he was going to take the child away from her... A choked sound emerged from her throat.

Luke was looking around the room, but, as if sensing her silent regard, he glanced directly at her. 'You find me uncouth and barbaric, Emmy. Is that why you ran out so dramatically?'

'I didn't think you'd notice,' she replied coldly. 'You were so busy.' So that had nettled him, had it? Not enough, she thought bitterly, to try and locate me. No, I bet he was too busy with another of his merry bloody widows, she thought viciously. Her dreams had been troubled by visions of Beth Urquhart.

'What,' he asked swiftly, a small crease between his darkly defined eyebrows, 'is that supposed to signify, or was it simply one of that plethora of childish retorts you have at your fingertips?'

'As if you didn't know,' she sneered.

He sat down on the sofa beside her, an arm laid across her shoulders effectively pinning her to the seat. She held herself rigid, swallowing hard as he pressed his thigh with slow deliberation against her own. 'I'm sure it's fascinating, but shall we get back to the original question? In case you've developed selective amnesia, Emily, I'll repeat myself,' he said with heavy irony. 'Are you carrying our child?' As he spoke he took her chin in his free hand and, fingertips pressing into the angle of her jaw, wrenched her head around until she had to meet his interrogative stare.

'*My* child,' she corrected, and her words lit a fire somewhere at the back of his eyes. 'How did you find out?'

Luke was silent for a long moment, as if he had trouble assimilating the information she had so reluctantly volunteered. The smile was silkily affable, his eyes hard and cold. 'One of life's little ironies, infant. Your father made sure I was there tonight.'

'I don't understand…'

'There's a lot of that going around, infant,' he shot back, his voice flecked with some of the rage that was obviously consuming him. 'Your dear papa made sure I'd be there tonight because I've been ignoring his recent phone calls. He wanted to read me a lecture on parental responsibility, would you believe? An incredible source to find such a doctrine preached,' he continued ironically. 'He accused me of deserting you like the worthless piece of scum I am. He waxed quite lyrical on the subject,' he recalled, with a satirical lift of an eyebrow. 'We exchanged some pleasantries and parted company.'

Emily saw no humour, not even of the ironical variety, in this information. Her mind was coming up against those dead ends again. The thought of her father confronting Luke made her imagination boggle. How on earth had he found out? 'You didn't hit him, did you?' Luke had such an air of suppressed violence about him that she could imagine her father pushing just that little too far. 'I don't understand. I haven't told him.'

'I didn't hit him, though the thought did cross my mind. You always did underestimate your father's ingenuity, infant. He's been tracking you since you got back to town. A visit to the local maternity clinic sort of gives massive clues.'

'That's disgusting!' she choked. The notion of being followed made her shudder.

'In the circumstances, I can only applaud the precaution-ary measure.'

'You're as bad as he is,' she said, incredulous at this peculiar alliance against her.

'He's only looking out for you, Emmy.'

'You're making excuses for my father,' she choked.

'I can understand the motivation,' he corrected quietly. 'You must be three months pregnant,' he added, making a swift mental calculation.

'Always assuming that the baby is yours.' Her face was a mask of unconcern. She could have told him to the day...to the hour how pregnant she was.

He took her by the shoulders and looked into her face, the blue eyes steadfast, the expression almost wary, tinged by a deep sadness that shone through the anger that was still etched in the tightly drawn lines of his face. She felt a fresh wave of bewilderment at his response. Had she half hoped he'd be willing to accept this simple get-out clause? It would be simpler for all concerned. She couldn't imagine Beth taking kindly to the situation.

'Are you going to tell me it's not?' His eyes slid to the flatness of her belly and back to her face. They glowed with a primitive possessiveness. 'I thought not,' he said with grim satisfaction as her expressive face confirmed what he was already sure of. 'Had you any intention of telling me?'

'No.'

An explosive sound escaped the confines of his chest. 'I suppose it's nothing to do with me.'

'You catch on so quickly,' she said admiringly.

'And you inhabit a fantasy world. Did you think your own family, living less than ten miles away, wouldn't no-tice when you produce a baby? How do you think I tracked you down here?' He gave a short, hard laugh. 'And to give the devil his due, he is genuinely concerned for your wel-fare. I think you actually scared him when you reacted the way you did to finding out about his little scam. It's probably the first time in his life he's felt guilt,' he added abruptly. He continued as she maintained a stunned silence. The flare of tenderness in his eyes had hit her in a vulnerable, exposed area. 'The fact that your mother would have a stroke if people knew she had a daughter bringing up a child in squalor virtually on her doorstep might have coloured the degree of his concern.' He clicked his tongue and shook his head. 'Bad for the image! Now, if it had been a designer drugs problem, that would be far more acceptable—one her cronies could identify with. It's almost obligatory in her circles.' His expression told her exactly what he thought of those circles. 'But poverty is just so unpicturesque.'

'This is not a hovel.' It hadn't been tenderness, she told herself, just her ever-hopeful imagination, a trick of the light. She wasn't going to build herself up to be smashed down.

'Depends how you look at it. As it happens, my child is not being brought up in some one-room attic.'

'It was good enough for you,' she bit back. Was he going to take everything from her—not just her love, the gift he had no need of, but the life born of that love too? She'd be damned before she was going to be pushed aside. She was genuinely confused. Luke seemed to want the child—in her mind she had never imagined that. Surely a baby would be an inconvenience? His lifestyle was not geared for parenthood; and besides, he and Beth had no more obstacles. Why create a new one?

'A situation I see no point in perpetuating,' he returned coldly. 'And the reason you're going to marry me.'

Emily gave a startled gasp. Not just the extraordinary thing he had just said robbed her of breath, but the way he'd said it, as though the matter were closed. 'I think you're the one inhabiting a fantasy world. I can do without your warped sense of honour, Luke Hunt.' She gave a laugh

that made the swift transition into choked sob, but her eyes
remained hard, not dewy. It hurt to be offered what she'd
dreamt of—marriage, a child—Luke's child—for all the
wrong reasons. 'What's wrong, Luke? Did Daddy tell you
to marry me? Or did he warn you not to? I suppose from
your point of view that's an attractive proposition. Well,
I'm no pawn to be sacrificed for either of you. I don't care
if my mother is the talk of the bridge club; this is my child
and legitimacy is not something I'm worried about. I know
all about loveless marriages, and I don't want one. Besides,
aren't you forgetting the delightful Beth?'

The colour seemed to be seeping from beneath Luke's
teak-dark tan as she spoke. He'd lost weight, she realised.
He'd always been lean, but the bones of his hawkish face
seemed more pronounced, the lines deeper ingrained. He
pushed his fingers through the thick pelt of his hair as he
spoke, and Emily was shocked somehow to see a few sil-
vered threads at his temple. Had he been ill? she wondered,
concern a pain in her belly.

'If you think for one moment I'll permit my child to be
raised by another man...' he said hoarsely.

'Does there always have to be a man?' she snapped.

The hand that went palm down, fingers splayed on her
stomach, made her flinch, but she couldn't move. Emotions
exploded within her at the gentle intimacy of the possessive
gesture. I won't cry, she thought, raising her frightened eyes
to his face... I won't.

'To be in this condition, Emmy...yes.' His eyes were
shadowed and turbulent. 'I'm sorry you find the idea of
matrimony so repugnant but I'll not settle for anything
less.' His expression was grim, totally unyielding. 'Besides,
it's me you need... I know it. Why do you have to deny
it constantly?'

'Your arrogance is pathetic.' Hot tears filled her eyes.
Was she really that transparent? she wondered with despair.
'What about Beth? How can you do this to her?'

Luke's expression grew intensely impatient. 'Why on earth do you keep throwing Beth in my face? Do you mind explaining just what the hell all these little digs are meant to indicate?'

Why did he have to keep up the façade? Would it last until he had given his child the legitimacy that obviously meant so much to him? 'I heard you and Beth at the flat,' she said, her eyes lowered, and she kept them fixed on her hands, which plucked restlessly at the hemline of her dress. 'I know you've been waiting for her to get over the death of her husband...to be together. I heard what she said. You were talking about her that day, weren't you? It would be—' she looked up, her eyes filled with the intensity of her feelings '—sinful to marry me, Luke, when you feel like that about someone else.'

She gave a sudden moan and pushed her head back into the sofa she'd so lovingly re-upholstered. 'This is such a mess. I know I should have told you about the baby,' she admitted with a rush. 'Marty kept nagging me to, but—'

'Who's Marty?' The ferocity was palpable.

She blinked. 'I'm having a baby...our baby.' It was the first time she'd said it and it felt right, good on her tongue, even though she knew it shouldn't. 'That doesn't give you the right to interrogate me about my friends.'

'Has he been here with you?' He looked around the room which had once seemed bright and cheerful but suddenly seemed cheap and sordid. Did he have to ruin everything?

'Marty is a female,' she said with a superior smile. 'Or had you hoped to have me labelled an unfit mother too?'

Luke seemed suddenly too pleased. The tension that had been part of him had been tight to snapping-point. It was still there, but he seemed more in control. 'I think you'll make an excellent mother, as a matter of fact. What I think is that you've got a generous heart that is longing to love, but no one's been around to return it, so you've hoarded it up until you've almost forgotten how to let it go. Until...'

His eyes were on her stricken face in which the colour welled and receded dramatically.

'Don't!' she begged. He knew she loved him. Her last defence was crumbling before her eyes.

'Emmy, my dear, stupid, blind infant.' He spoke in such a tender, loving tone that her eyes grew round in response to the trauma of the endearing insult to her nervous system. 'You ran out on me because you imagined Beth and I were in love.'

'I heard—' she began indignantly. He wasn't going to dismiss the weeks of suffering with some glib comment. This was some plan to take away her baby.

'You heard part of a conversation,' he interrupted, the anger close again to the surface. 'As always, you believed what you wanted about me. If you'd stayed around to eavesdrop further—'

'You kissed her!' Emily exploded wrathfully. My God, do I really sound that jealous? she thought, hearing the sound of her own voice with subdued shock. 'I saw you,' she added in a more moderate tone.

'What you saw was me being kissed.'

'In fact, you were overcome and taken by force,' she snapped. 'All six feet three of you!'

A strange smile lurked around the corners of his mouth. 'This jealousy is something of a revelation, Emmy. Now just shut up and listen for a moment.' He pressed a finger to her lips and something in his eyes made her grow still. 'I've known Beth since she married Martin, several years ago. They enjoyed a stormy relationship but were, despite the intermittent volcanic disturbances, very happy. When Martin was killed Beth went totally off the rails. For weeks she refused even to believe Martin was dead. The anger and the guilt that followed in its wake were frightening to watch. I was a friend, nothing more.' He glanced at her intent face, his expression uncomfortable for the first time. 'It seems—and I blame myself for not realising it—that I became more to Beth than an outlet for the pain that was tearing her apart. I've been encouraging her for the last twelve months to do what she really wants and move back to London. She ran her own advertising company until she made the move up north. I was pleased that she felt able to make the break, rebuild her life, but I hadn't bargained on being part of the package.'

Relief was swimming through her veins. It was the truth, a truth that suddenly made the present difficult to evaluate accurately. Concepts were shifting. 'You were with her tonight.'

'You were with Gavin,' he reminded her with compelling anger.

'We have settled our differences,' she agreed. 'We're friends, and we'll never be anything else—unless he's my brother-in-law. I was a last-minute sub for Charlotte tonight. They had a slight disagreement.'

'And I was there because your father sent me a very terse missive strictly forbidding me to put in an appearance,' he told her, a flare of satisfaction curving his mouth at her explanation. 'Beth, on the other hand, was present because she is involved with the charity that organised the damned thing. In the circumstances she has taken it very well. I think seeing you at the flat cleared her vision—she was just reluctant to let go of the fantasy. There never were any sparks between us, and you can't manufacture that sort of thing. I was a crutch for Beth and possibly I let her lean on me too heavily,' he said, his voice filled with self-doubt. 'It was a pretty delicate half-hour, but I think we salvaged our friendship.' With a sudden violent movement he grabbed Emily's hands and drew her towards him on the small sofa. 'And then I came to find you packing your bags,' he told her grimly.

'Luke,' she said suddenly, a dazed expression in her eyes, 'why did you let me go?' Her voice became hoarse with urgency. Her eyes, the dark brown speckled with golden highlights, were fixed unblinkingly on his face.

The blue eyes she loved so much, the ones that seemed to see inside her head, were glittering with feverish intensity. 'It hurt to know that despite how close I had thought we were at times you could still distrust me so totally.' The beads of sweat that shone on his brow increased the impression of the phenomenal strain he seemed to be feeling. She saw the muscles in his throat stand out as he swallowed an invisible constriction. 'I didn't come after you tonight just because of the baby, or at your father's bidding. I came because...because I had to.' His hands, for once clumsy and ill co-ordinated, fumbled as they moved up the length of her arms and down her back, tightening painfully around her ribs. His head dropped to lie against the angle of her shoulder, his breath hot on the skin of her neck. 'God, you feel...' A ragged cry was wrenched from deep inside him as his mouth moved across her skull. She felt the pressure of his lips through the cap of her hair.

Her own movements were made difficult by the violent tremors which began to afflict her entire body. The same tremors, she realised with a dawning wonder, that were shaking Luke's larger frame with equal fury. His body was all hard muscle, taut, so strong, yet he was trembling.

Hesitantly her arms went up around him, moving over his broad back—at first tentatively, but with growing confidence as she grew greedy for the closeness, the sharing of something she could find no name for. She'd been saying his name repeatedly in a tone half between a sob and a question when she became aware of his stillness.

Luke raised his head from its resting place. 'How could you think I was in love with Beth after we had made love?' he demanded angrily.

What was he saying? She hardly noticed the cruel grip of his fingers as they dug into her upper arms. 'I was just there and you kept harping on about propinquity. You made no secret of the fact that half my attraction was due to my being a means of revenge. Then after Beth turned up you virtually rubbed my nose in the great power that special woman had over you.'

'A special woman,' he said thickly. '*You*, Emily Ruth Stapely—the only woman I have ever loved.' He gave a sudden deep laugh at the totally incredulous expression on her face. 'You look as though you're about to say this is so sudden.'

'You hate my father, despise my family,' she protested weakly.

He didn't attempt to deny it. 'That's one reason I put myself through hell trying to deny the obvious. Don't you think I tried to dislike you, believe every rotten thing I accused you of? Me, fall for a Stapely? Even when you were a kid I knew you were different, and you have no idea how terrifying you were at sixteen, all seductive promise and endless trust.' He shook his head. 'I'm ashamed to say how tempting you were, little one. I had to keep reminding myself that despite outward appearances you were still a child. I was pretty disgusted with myself. Why the hell do you think I stayed clear for four years? I could only trust my good intentions at a safe distance,' he recalled wryly. He smiled at her and there was no hidden agenda, just warmth and passion and possession. 'I feel as if in some strange way the outcome was never in question.'

He ran his fingers down the side of her face, the tips rough against the silky texture. 'Why do you think I came back in time for your party? It wasn't coincidence. Maybe I was in love with you even then,' he reflected in a startled tone. 'I didn't want to fall in love with a Stapely. My hate for your family has coloured my every waking moment. I didn't want to see you as an individual who was as much a victim of your birth as I was.'

His thumb blotted a solitary tear that ran down the smoothness of her cheek. 'I was in this tropical paradise,' he recalled, 'Then a single line in a letter from a friend in England stole my peace of mind away.' His eyes raked her face. 'Your wedding plans. I knew it was totally unreasonable but I was furious. I spent the next week carping, ranting about the ridiculous idea of the whole affair. I couldn't get it out of my head. When Bernie Cavanaugh, who is a very shrewd lady, asked me if it was marriage in particular, the bridegroom, or you being other than single which bothered me so much, I had no answer, so she said it might be a good idea if I found out before it was too late.

'I didn't think when you walked in on that farcical, furtive scene, I just acted on pure instinct. I knew I had to get you away from that bloody family of yours if we were going to get anywhere. I played up to your preconceptions about me. If I'd actually told you the truth, you'd either have run a mile or laughed in my face. I just knew I had to have you, and if that involved fulfilling my role as unscrupulous bastard I was going to do it. To be honest, I still had hopes that I could work through this obsession, that I could rid my bloodstream of the ridiculous craving. But I admitted defeat fairly swiftly,' he told her self-consciously. 'I took comfort from the fact that your physical response to me was no illusion. I thought if we were together long enough I could teach you to love me too. I know my methods were hardly scrupulous...'

A flood of joy was spilling out of her; a new confidence swelled and grew as he spoke. 'I'm glad you didn't find a cure for the obsession,' she said firmly. Her eyes glowed as she placed her hands on either side of his face. 'I love you, Luke, and I feel ashamed I didn't have the guts to tell you so. I misjudged you, but when you've been fed information about a person all your life the ideas are hard to dislodge.' Her face creased in anguish. 'You never told me, never even hinted. I thought I was a form of retribution, Luke, a pawn in some deadly game. You spoilt me for anyone else when I fell for you at sixteen. You must know that.'

His eyes darkened in anguish. 'Emily, I told you in every way I could.'

'Except in words.'

He nodded in acquiescence. 'Except in words. Perhaps we were both afraid of rejection.'

The concept of Luke feeling as vulnerable and unsure as she had, suffering the same torture, was shattering. 'I'll always be my father's daughter, Luke; you'll never be able to forget that,' she said with a shade of unease that dimmed the joy she'd felt.

'My wife first,' he said with the arrogant tilt to his head which she loved. But the melting tenderness was new, and it was for her. 'I'm not marrying your father. Do you realise that in his own way he was acting as matchmaker today? In the circumstances he can't object to our marriage, can he? Actually, he admitted a few things today that almost explain...not excuse, but explain. He was in love with my mother.' He gave an ironic grin as Emily's jaw fell open. 'My reaction exactly. She apparently would have none of it, but he had hopes until my father came along. I look like my father, it seems. End of story.'

'That's no excuse,' she objected. 'If this baby—' she touched her stomach '—were another man's, you wouldn't take out your frustration on him.'

'No, Emily I wouldn't,' he agreed quietly. 'That's an impressive piece of faith, infant.' The pleasure he felt at her swift response rounded the gravelly edges of his voice. 'But I'd never let another man steal you from me,' he warned her huskily.

'You didn't follow me,' she reminded him.

'Pride,' he said in a clipped tone, 'has made the last months a living hell. I'd almost given up fighting, waiting for you to make the first move. Hell, Emmy, no proper explanation...you just ran. I thought you couldn't stand the sight of me. I knew, though, that you couldn't have been so sweet, so wonderful when we made love if there were nothing. I clung on to that and waited stubbornly for you to make the first move. I'd have done anything to make you mine, and I still would.' Anguish, the shadow of nightmares, twisted his features. 'It's been a nightmare wanting you, trying to convince myself you weren't worth all the agonies. I thought you might have found someone else... Emmy, I was touched, flattered that I was your first. But it's the last I want to be.'

His lips were hungry, drinking her in like a man who'd spent days in a desert. She pressed eagerly closer, feeling the same urgency flood her veins.

When they eventually broke apart, they were both gasping for air. 'The baby, Emmy—how do you feel about it?' Luke asked.

'When I thought it was all I had of you, or ever would have, the baby was everything to me. Now you and the baby are my world. And you?'

'I'm filled with a proprietorial delight at the prospect of watching you grow fat and gorgeous with the seed of life we began.' He shifted his weight and leant back, pulling her half on top of him. 'Is there much evidence of occupation yet?' he asked curiously, stroking her flat belly.

'I'll let you decide that, darling,' she said with a small, provocative smile.

'I think I can handle that,' he murmured receptively, and the hungry prowling of his eyes over her body made her quiver in anticipation. 'Em, back in Scotland, a million years or so ago, I thought you might be holding back because of my line of work. You know, war zones.'

'Civil wars, famine,' she added stoically. 'I don't want to change you, tie you down,' she said, trying to ignore the cold fingers of dread that clutched at her heart. To lose Luke... But to tether him was equally unthinkable.

'I'm not addicted to danger, Emily. To be honest, being

a voyeur, an observer, on the depths of human misery can have a seriously numbing effect on the body—not to mention the mind. My life has been out of balance and I reached my limit a while back. I've curtailed my activities in that field recently.'

Emily's eyes grew soft and dark as she was filled with a rush of tenderness. 'What happened?'

He shook his head. 'Not now, honey,' he said roughly. 'I don't want anything dark to get in the way. Let's just say I had nightmares for a good six months, and pictures that played incessantly in my head. As a photographer, reporter, or whatever, the main feeling is of impotence. Sometimes we help by focusing the world's eyes on atrocities, but on the immediate level we can only watch. You can't afford to lose that protective veneer of objectivity. I'm telling you this, love, in case you're afraid I'll do anything to jeopardise what we have,' he explained, tenderly touching her soft mouth with his fingertip, tracing the outline.

'I'm not afraid, Luke,' she said slowly, moved almost to tears by his words. 'Not with you, my love.'

'Do you know how badly I need you, Emmy mine?' he asked huskily.

'Show me,' she suggested imperiously. An order he didn't appear to mind obeying at all.

The world's bestselling romance series.

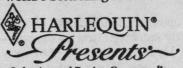

HARLEQUIN®
Presents

Seduction and Passion Guaranteed!

Introducing Jane Porter's exciting new series

**The Galván men: proud Argentine aristocrats...
who've chosen American rebels as their brides!**

IN DANTE'S DEBT
Harlequin Presents #2298

Count Dante Galván was ruthless—and though it broke Daisy's
heart she had no alternative but to hand over control of her family's
stud farm to him. She was in Dante's debt up to her ears! Daisy
knew she was far too ordinary ever to become the count's wife—
but could she resist his demands that she repay her dues in his bed?

On sale January 2003

LAZARO'S REVENGE
Harlequin Presents #2304

Lazaro Herrera has vowed revenge on Dante, his half brother, who
refuses to acknowledge his existence. When Dante's sister-in-law
Zoe arrives in Argentina, it seems the perfect opportunity. But
the clash of Zoe's blond and blue-eyed beauty with his own
smoldering dark looks creates a sexual force so strong that
Lazaro's plan begins to fall apart....

On sale February 2003

**Pick up a Harlequin Presents® novel and you will enter
a world of spine-tingling passion and
provocative, tantalizing romance!**

Available wherever Harlequin books are sold.

HARLEQUIN®
Makes any time special ®

Visit us at www.eHarlequin.com

HPGALVAN

International bestselling author

SANDRA MARTON

invites you to attend the

WEDDING *of the* YEAR

Glitz and glamour prevail in this volume
containing a trio of stories in which
three couples meet at a
high society wedding—and
soon find themselves
walking down the aisle!

Look for it in November 2002.

HARLEQUIN®
Makes any time special®

$ Saving Money $ Has Never Been This Easy!

Just fill out and send in this form from any October, November and December 2002 books and we will send you a coupon booklet worth a total savings of $20.00 off future purchases of Harlequin and Silhouette books in 2003.

Yes! It's that easy!

I accept your incredible offer!
Please send me a coupon booklet:

Name (PLEASE PRINT)

Address   Apt. #

City   State/Prov.   Zip/Postal Code

In a typical month, how many
Harlequin and Silhouette novels do you read?

❏ **0-2**   ❏ **3+**

097KJKDNC7   097KJKDNDP

Please send this form to:
 In the U.S.: Harlequin Books, P.O. Box 9071, Buffalo, NY 14269-9071
 In Canada: Harlequin Books, P.O. Box 609, Fort Erie, Ontario L2A 5X3

Allow 4-6 weeks for delivery. Limit one coupon booklet per household. Must be postmarked no later than January 15, 2003.

HARLEQUIN®
Makes any time special®

Silhouette®
Where love comes alive™